ROYAL SHARK

KYLIE GILMORE

Royal Shark © 2019 by Kylie Gilmore

First Edition: August 2019

Cover design by Michele Catalano Creative

Published by: Extra Fancy Books

ISBN-10: 1-947379-00-3

ISBN-13: 978-1-947379-00-8

Once upon a time they made a pact to marry when they were 25…
They're now 25.

1

———

The Pact

Thirteen years ago…

Adrian

"I bet you're too chicken to race to the big rock!" The big rock is much farther than we usually swim. I rip off my T-shirt, tossing it on the sand. I've got her. Sara Travers can't resist a bet.

She stands in her blue swimsuit and plants her hands on her hips, making the bottom of her tank lift. "You wish, Adrian!"

I stare at her smooth tanned stomach, and I get this *feeling*. I've been getting it all summer whenever her top lifts. It's strange because it's the same stomach and curve of lower back I saw last summer and all the summers before. It must mean I'm ready for a girlfriend like my older brothers. I am twelve, practically a teenager, and being the youngest, I've always worked hard to keep up with my four older brothers. Oscar told me it's easy to get a girlfriend. As soon as they hear you're a prince, they practically throw themselves at your feet.

She marches up to me, her long blond hair swinging in a

high ponytail, her green eyes flashing. "I bet I win the race, sucker!"

Then again, I may have known her too long for the prince thing to have any effect. Me, Sara, and my twin, Silvia, have spent every summer together since we were eight. Sara's father is from France and used to visit Villroy as a child. That's why they rent a cottage here. Her mother is American, so they live back in New York City.

I smirk. "Here's the bet. When I win, you give me your cookies for the rest of the week." Her mother bakes chocolate chip cookies and sends them in Sara's packed lunch on beach days. We never get those at the palace. Sara only shares a tiny crumb normally.

She crinkles her nose, the sprinkle of light freckles across it catching my eye. There's seven freckles, my lucky number. "When *I* win, I want dibs on the front seat for the rest of the week."

Usually I get the front seat of the car because I'm the tallest at five feet nine. Silvia, Sara, and Sara's little sister, Chloe, get the backseat. Our driver/guard picks them up and drops them off at their place. There's a second car with another guard and Silvia's maid, Marie, who is *not* a babysitter for us. Marie keeps an eye on Chloe, who's a five-year-old terror.

"Hi-yah!" Chloe shouts at the top of her lungs and then kicks her way through the sand castle that Silvia spent the last hour helping her make.

"Chloe!" Silvia exclaims, plucking Chloe up and out of the way.

"I'm Godzilla!" Chloe shouts, kicking wildly. Her ponytail band must've lost its grip because all I see is a crazy blur of blond hair.

Sara shakes her head. "I told you she'd destroy it."

Silvia puts Chloe down, who goes right back to destroying the sand castle with wild kicks and karate chops. Silvia sighs. "I made it extra special, too, with a moat and everything."

"You wanna race me and Adrian?" Sara asks. "Winner gets the front seat."

"I'm going to read," Silvia says and takes a seat under the white canvas cabana. Her dark brown hair hangs straight to her shoulders instead of in the neat bun our mother insists on. Lately, Silvia has been making "personal fashion choices" away from the palace. I'll never tell. We're closer than best friends, being twins.

We're on the north shore beach, which is great because of all the fish. Anyone could come here since it's a public beach, but they usually go for the south side beaches closer to the port, where the public ferry comes in.

"Come on," I say to Sara, heading toward the water.

"Don't you think Silvia reads too much?" Sara whispers as soon as we're a distance away. "I only read on rainy days and during school when they make me."

I lift one shoulder. My twin has always been a big reader. I like math a lot better; numbers always make sense.

We wade in up to our knees, the waves splashing us. Sara turns to me, a gleam in her eye. She thinks she can win. "On the count of three."

I nod once.

She narrows her eyes, looking at our goal, the big black rock. "One."

I crouch low, ready to dive under the waves.

"Two." *Splash!* She went on two!

I dive in after her, swimming furiously to catch up to her. I should've known she'd cheat. She wants to win as bad as I do.

I pull ahead easily. My arms and legs are longer, and my shoulders are bigger and stronger now that I had a growth spurt. I slow down, keeping pace with her so she'll feel like she has a chance. I'll pull ahead at the very last minute. Girls hate when you win by too much. My twin taught me that.

I swim, keeping her in sight. Waiting…waiting…now! I pull ahead and claim the victory. I wait for her to lift her head and realize her loss before punching a hand in the air. "I won, you little cheater!"

She treads water. "Your arms are longer. It wasn't a fair race unless I had a head start."

"Mmm, can't wait to eat all those cookies. Don't worry, I'll give you a chip."

"Joke's on you. I can just eat some at home."

I hadn't thought of that. It's not as great a victory as I hoped. "Who cares? I still won."

We float in silence on our backs for a bit. She's not like her little sister, always chattering. Thankfully.

After a while, she straightens, treading water. I tread water too. I'm about to ask if she wants to go double or nothing on a race back to shore when she says, "I think my parents are going to get a divorce."

This is a shock. Whenever her parents join us on the beach, they always seem so happy, joking around and holding hands. "Why do you think that?"

"They've been arguing a lot."

"About what?"

Her lips form a flat line. "My dad wants to quit his job and start his own company. My mom says it's not a good time."

"That's not too bad. I'm sure they'll figure it out. They still hold hands, right?"

"Not really."

"Oh." I don't know what to say. I hope she's wrong. "I'm sure it'll be fine."

"You don't know that."

I change tactics. "I *bet* you it'll be fine. By next summer, they'll be back to normal. I'll give you my dragon cards if I lose the bet, which I won't." It's my best playing card set, with detailed dragon illustrations on the back, which I know is her favorite.

She tries to smile but can't manage it. "Wanna race back? Double or nothing."

I grin. "I'll even give you a three-second head start."

Her green eyes light up. "Go!"

I watch her swim, counting extra slow.

"Ah!" She jackknifes upright suddenly and then drops like a stone underwater.

I swim to her, and she pops up again. "My ankle! It hurts so bad." She starts to sink again.

I grab her arm, keeping her above water. "Float on your back. What happened?"

"I think I cut it on a rock." She lifts her ankle above the water, and blood drips out of a gash in it. That looks really bad. "Oh my God! I'm going to bleed out, surrounded by sharks, who'll eat my leg, and then I'll drown!"

I'm already thinking ahead to getting her to shore before she loses too much blood. "The sharks aren't going to eat you. We don't have sharks."

"Yes, you do! Sharks can go anywhere!"

"Do the backstroke and try not to kick that leg too much. I'll swim back with you."

"I'm scared," she says in a small voice.

"I'll tow you." I wrap an arm around her middle, prepared to pull her to shore.

"No, I can do it. Just keep talking to me, okay? Distract me."

So I do. I swim freestyle with my head above water, telling her how much I want to go off island for school next year to get better teachers for math, how I want to go to Cambridge, which is the best for math, and how I'll learn all about statistics, so I'll always know the best odds and beat everyone at poker. My father taught me and my brothers to play poker when each of us turned seven because he thought it was a good way to learn numbers and people skills at the same time. I think he just wanted a game we could all have fun with. It was a father-son thing, but I taught my twin and Sara, too, so they'd play with me.

"You'll have to teach me all your best poker tricks," she says weakly.

Panic shoots through me. She never sounds weak. I fear she's lost too much blood. "Almost there."

Finally, we get to a point where I can stand. I scoop her up and carry her to the beach.

"Help!" I shout.

My guard, Thomas, runs over and takes her from me. She stares at me over his shoulder, her eyes begging me to stay with her. I glance at her ankle, still dripping blood, and race for my T-shirt on the sand. I shake it out, turn it inside out, and then tie it over her ankle to stem the blood flow. She makes a strangled noise at the contact. Blood starts to soak through the shirt.

"Oh!" Marie, our maid, exclaims as everyone gathers around Sara. "That's going to need stitches."

"Stitches!" Sara exclaims. "No-o-o! Please no stitches!"

Thomas rushes off with her in his arms, heading for the car.

"I'll get her mother," Marie says. "Come on, everyone, we're going to pick up Sara's mother and meet them at the health clinic."

"Adrian!" Sara yells.

I run to her. "It's okay. It won't be that bad."

Her eyes are so wide I can see the whites in them. "I don't want a needle in my ankle! It's already ripped open!"

"You have to," I say. "It'll be okay."

"Don't leave me," she whispers.

"I won't."

I climb into the backseat with her on the drive to the clinic. Thomas and Marie have a quick talk about whether or not Marie should ride in the back with us to apply pressure to Sara's ankle, but Sara says she'll do it. She doesn't want anyone touching her injury. A moment later, we're heading to the clinic, just me and Sara in the backseat, with Thomas driving. The others follow in the second car. Sara looks really pale.

I do my best to make her feel better. "Oscar got stitches in his arm and it was cool. It looked like Frankenstein."

"I don't want to look like Frankenstein!" she wails.

I wince. "Not Frankenstein. Just cool. And it didn't even hurt. They numbed his arm first."

"They did?"

"Yeah."

"Like with a special numbing cream?"

I debate what to say. Oscar said it was a huge needle. Finally, I say, "They can't put cream on an open wound. It's just a quick shot of medicine."

She grabs my hand and squeezes tight.

I stare straight ahead. I've never held hands with a girl before. It kind of hurts.

"Keep talking," she says.

"About what?"

"I don't care. I just like the sound of your voice."

It is deeper now. I lower it to an even deeper tone. "Remember when Chloe was two and she kept ripping off her swim diaper and leaping into the waves?"

She laughs a little. "Yeah. My parents were so tired of trying to keep her safe and clean."

"And then she got sunburn on her butt." I laugh. "That should've taught her a lesson, but she just wouldn't stop." I glance over to see Sara looking more relaxed, so I keep it up with the Chloe stories. There's plenty of them, and it is pretty funny looking back. At the time, the three of us older kids just thought Chloe was a pain, distracting from the real plans for the day.

A short while later, we arrive at the clinic and Sara is rushed inside, where her mother is waiting. I'm not allowed in the back room with her, so I follow Thomas to the car, hoping she's okay.

It's the last day before Sara leaves Villroy. We've spent the last three weeks playing poker, either under the cabana on the beach or, on bad weather days, at the palace in the salon, which is my favorite room because it's the most relaxed with a leather sofa. Sara could've went back to swimming after her stitches were out, but she didn't want to go in the water. I think she's afraid of it now. All she wants to do is play poker. We bet with Monopoly money, but the stakes feel real. We're both competitive and both love to win. Sometimes Silvia plays with us or one of my brothers, but mostly it's just me and Sara. We've been playing with my dragon cards, and I plan to give them to her as a gift to take home with her. She always admires them, and they don't have anything like it where she's from. I've been waiting for the perfect moment.

Silvia pokes her head in the cabana. "Chloe wants to ride bikes again. You coming?"

"We're in the middle of a game," Sara says, studying her cards.

"You're supposed to be *my* best friend," Silvia says tightly.

I look up, and Silvia glares at me. "Sil, she's both of our friends. What's the big deal? She doesn't want to go bike riding."

"Sara," Silvia says through her teeth, "may I speak to you outside?"

Sara stands, tucking her cards against her body so I can't see them, and joins Silvia outside the cabana. I can still hear them. The cabana is canvas not actual walls.

"I thought you were my best friend," Silvia says.

"I *am* your best friend," Sara says. "I just don't want to ride bikes. My ankle is still healing."

"Your ankle is fine," Silvia snaps. "You rode earlier. Why don't you just admit you like Adrian?"

Interesting. I suspected as much. Ever since I helped Sara through her ankle injury, she's been looking at me like I'm her hero. I did save her in a way, helping her keep a level head and safely get out of the water. Maybe she's ready for a boyfriend. I'm definitely ready for a girlfriend. Only problem is I won't see her for a whole year after this.

"I do not," Sara protests hotly.

"Yes, you do. Ever hear sisters before misters?"

"No."

"That means you don't drop your friends because you like a boy."

"I don't *like* him!"

"Then why do you spend all of your time with him?"

"We always invite you to play with us."

Silvia snorts. "I don't like poker. It's boring."

"It's not. You can win big. It's so fun!"

"Win play money? Big deal."

Silence. A very long silence. Just when I think they've walked away, my sister pipes up.

"Fine," Silvia says. "Enjoy your stupid game with your boyfriend."

"I will!" Sara calls. "And he's not my boyfriend!"

She appears in the cabana, her cheeks flushed pink, and takes her seat. "I don't know what her problem is."

"It's a twin thing. She wants girls to spend more time with her than her boy twin, but sometimes the boy twin is kind of a hero." I grin, and she laughs.

We go back to playing. It gets quiet as everyone takes off on a bike ride.

We play several hands until Sara wins the pot. She's so happy she stops to count all her play money before hugging it to her, a huge beaming smile on her face.

I find myself smiling back even though I lost. I really like seeing her so happy.

Our eyes lock for a long moment before I return my attention to the cards. I'm pretty sure she *likes* me. I gather the cards into a neat stack and clear my throat. "Here." I offer them to her. "A gift for your last day here."

She sets the play money down and stares at the cards and then at me. "That's so nice, but I can't take your cards. They're special. You said you got them for Christmas."

"That's why I want you to have them. You know they're special and will take good care of them." I press them into her hand, and her fingers close around them.

"Thank you." She takes a deep breath. "You *are* my hero, Adrian. When I cut my ankle, I could've been eaten by sharks, drowned in my own panic, or bled out on the beach, but you *saved* me. You helped me through a major freak-out, so thank you times a gazillion."

My chest puffs with pride. I love being a hero. Being the youngest in the family, there was never a chance to be one. "You're welcome."

She looks up at me under her lashes, and my heart kicks harder. "I want to marry you when I grow up."

My eyes widen. Married? I thought maybe she'd be my girlfriend for a day before she left. *Married?*

She leans forward. "If we got married, we could play poker all night, every night."

That seals it for me. All poker all the time? Deal me in. She's the ideal opponent, as into the game as I am.

"Deal," I say.

"Great! Let's make a pact."

"A pact." That sounds more serious than a promise. "How should we seal the deal? A blood oath?"

She shudders. "No." She sets the dragon cards down on the smoothed-out sand playing area between us and fans them out. "When we're twenty-five, we'll get married. That'll give us time to go to college and get good jobs."

That's thirteen years away, double our lives now. "It sounds so far away. Are you sure you won't forget me?" I'm teasing. We've known each other much too long to ever forget.

She nods once, taking me seriously. "That's why we'll each take a pair, twos and fives, to remind us of the proper age, hearts and diamonds of course. Then when we reunite, we'll have a matched set of two and five—two hearts, two diamonds just like a wedding."

"Guys don't wear diamonds. I'll get you a ring with two diamonds."

"Okay," she says softly.

She takes a two of hearts and a two of diamonds for herself and gives me a five of hearts and a five of diamonds. "You get the higher cards since you're older." My birthday is five months before hers. She holds up her cards. "Now we both have a pair, but together it unlocks the magic combination of twenty-five."

She's so smart. And her green eyes sparkle. And she has a sprinkle of freckles across her nose that exactly matches my lucky number.

"The two and five together make seven," I tell her. "That's my lucky number. Maybe you're good luck too because you have seven freckles on your nose."

She covers her nose with her hand. "I hate my freckles."

"I don't." I pull her hand away from her face. She's so pretty I find myself leaning closer and then I know what I really want. "I bet you're too chicken to kiss me."

Her lips part in surprise before she quickly recovers. "I bet *you're* too chicken to kiss *me*."

"I'm not."

She licks her lips. "Then prove it."

"You have to get closer."

She shifts the cards out of the way and kneels on our playing area. I kneel too, the pair of cards slipping from my hand in my excitement. My heart races.

"I've never been kissed before," she whispers.

Neither have I, but I'm her hero and need to stay that way. "Don't worry, I know what I'm doing." I've spied on my oldest brother Gabriel. The trick is you have to hold the girl's face so you don't miss her lips. "Close your eyes." That's the other important part.

She's so close I can feel her breathy response warm over my lips. "Why?"

"That's how it works."

She gazes into my eyes, and the blood rushes through my veins. "I want to see you."

I hold her face with both hands, surprised at how soft her skin is. Our eyes meet up close. I can't blink, the green of her eyes mesmerizing me. And then, finally, I close the distance, pressing my lips to hers, shocked at the jolt that runs through me at contact.

I drop my hands and lean back. I want to know if she liked it as much as I did, but I can't ask. Instead, I study her expression, which looks intensely thoughtful. Her cheeks are light pink. I'm not sure if she's embarrassed or happy, like me.

And then she smiles, and I can breathe again.

She gathers up the dragon cards, minus my pair of fives, and tucks them into her backpack. Then she stands and hooks the backpack over her shoulder, her expression serious. "I'm definitely going to marry you, Adrian Rourke."

She takes off.

I grin. I must be a fantastic kisser.

Wait. Where did she go? I step out of the cabana. Her backpack is on the sand, and she's splashing in the shallows. I strip off my T-shirt and join her, glad she's not afraid of the water anymore.

She splashes me, laughing, and I splash her back. She dives under a wave, and I join her, swimming out to calmer waters.

She's my girlfriend, my first girlfriend, my first kiss. I'll always remember this day, and I'll honor our pact because that's what heroes do.

2

———

Present day

Adrian

Opening and running a successful casino takes three things—brains, money, customer relations. I'm working all three. I would like to be just the brains, dealing with the numbers, and leave the rest to someone else. That's my strength. I have two silent partners who are also the money—my sister Emma and her husband, rock star Jackson Walker. I invested one-third of the start-up costs myself; they contributed the other two-thirds. They're both musicians living in nearby France, who perform here regularly, but they're not interested in the day-to-day running of the casino and leave all the decision-making to me. It sounds ideal, I know, but one month out from the opening of our new casino, Villroy Palace Casino, and I'm already wishing I had someone to take some of the heavy load off my shoulders. I'm not opposed to hard work. I'm opposed to round-the-clock work, especially when it comes to customer relations and staff management. Being the youngest of seven, I'm used to a crowd. I'm just not used to that crowd always needing something from me.

I step into the lobby of the casino at ten thirty in the morning, half an hour before opening, and smile to myself. I love the way the casino turned out. It was my idea to open a casino as a complement to our day spa, which opened a year ago. I'm a card shark. Monte Carlo was my second home for high-stakes poker, and now Villroy has its own version of Monte Carlo—a small but luxurious place meant to attract high rollers.

The front lobby is reminiscent of the Island Bliss Spa just across the way, with a matching decorative wall featuring a trickling waterfall, white tile floor, and white walls. The air is scented with lavender just like the spa. The idea was to make spa visitors continue their relaxed feel when they stepped over here. Where the reception desk would be at the spa, we have a fanciful glass sculpture of a dragon on top of a circular deep red rug with a tree branch pattern that's a reference to Yggdrasil, the world tree in Norse, a nod to the Rourkes' Viking heritage. I've always liked dragons, part of Viking mythology. There's also decorative Viking shields, swords, and tapestries with ancient battle symbols as wall decorations. We're descended from a renegade Viking tribe known as the Wild Ones. Vikings were risk takers, so I like the subtle nudge to our customers to take a risk too with their gambling. What fun is gambling without the heart-pounding excitement of the risk involved? I never played for the money. It was always for the adrenaline rush.

The gaming areas are visible just through twin archways on either side of the dragon sculpture. The casino itself is decorated in an elegant nineteenth-century style similar to Amalie Palace, where the royal family, including me, lives. I step through the archway into the main gambling hall with a ceiling painted to look like the sky, subtly backlit. The walls are done in sea green silk wallpaper with gold leaf, and the gaming tables are mahogany surrounded by red velvet chairs. There's a back wall of windows offering a spectacular view of the sea. We don't keep gamblers in the dark here. A slot machine room is tucked into a corner on the left, the money room in the middle, and my office is on the right. Upstairs are the high-roller private lounges, a small venue for performers that can double as a private gambling space, and an upscale seafood restaurant with a bar. In good weather, the roof terrace is used for performances and exclusive high-stakes games.

I take in the activity as I work my way toward my office. Dealers are setting up at the tables. Someone on the custodial staff is making one last sweep of the room. Security is gathered in a clump by the windows. So far, so good.

"Good morning, Denis," I call to the middle-aged man setting up for blackjack closest to my office.

He snaps to attention and bows his head. "Good morning, Your Highness."

That's another issue. Most of the staff are deferential to my title—Prince Adrian Rourke at your service—and it makes it more difficult to get to the heart of problems. They don't want to trouble me with the mundane. For example, the malfunctioning slot machine that kept eating tokens but stopped spinning. One dealer left his post to find a technician rather than call me. You cannot leave a gaming table full of chips in the middle of a game!

"Just Adrian will suffice," I say with what I hope is a disarming smile. "How's the blackjack table?"

"No trouble at all, sir."

"Good. We'll be rotating you to a poker table next week just to keep things fresh."

"As you wish, sir."

I continue to my office. I am CEO, CFO, the marketing guy, the HR guy, and the pit boss. My staff consists of dealers, money changers, technicians, janitors, waiters, bartenders, the chef and his assistant cooks, and security. A lot of security. What I need most at this point is a pit boss to oversee the staff, whom they'll feel more comfortable going to for problems. A right-hand man or woman, someone sharp who knows gambling as well as I do, someone relatable. It's not like I'm a snob, above it all. It's having a prince as a boss that's the problem. I may have been raised in the royal family but we're a rather down-to-earth lot, if you ask me. Plus I always had my twin sister, Silvia, to keep me from getting a big head about anything. Nothing like a sister to cut you down to size.

My assistant, Jean-Luc, who works in the small office connected to mine, pops his blond head in. He's twenty, a native of Villroy from a long line of fishermen. He's thrilled to have an office job. His father didn't mind since he also left the fishing trade to work on the cosmetics manufacturing line we have now on Villroy, working with more profitable fish oil. Jean-Luc is organized and neat from his perfectly groomed hair in a short cut with spikes in front to his neatly pressed short-sleeved pink shirt with beige trousers. "Good morning, Adrian."

I told him on his first day that if he didn't call me by my name instead of Your Highness, I'd fire him. I said it with a smile so he wouldn't be worried. I need the person working with me most to relax around me. "Good morning, Jean-Luc. What's the latest?"

He recites the list. "You need to go over payroll and sign off on it, there's an issue with a new employee who apparently forged their work visa, the weekend bartender quit, and security believes they found a cheating couple in last night's poker game."

I clench my jaw. "Why didn't security come to me last night about the cheaters?"

He pulls at his collar and swallows visibly, his Adam's apple bobbing up and down. "They feared rushing to an accusation, especially with new guests, so they thought they'd have you review the video this morning and give your opinion."

I lift my palms. "What does it matter now? They've probably already left the island." We cater to day-trippers. There's no hotel here.

He backs up a step and then another, inching toward the door. Obviously, I need to temper my tone of voice. I may be six feet with a muscular build that gets a rigorous workout sparring with the palace guards, but I'm not going to throttle my assistant.

I take a deep breath. I don't mean to sound like a snarling boss. I'm normally a low-key, mellow person. I've even been called a gentleman for my excellent manners and consideration of women. My twin taught me a lot about the care and feeding of women. Ha! Never tangle with a hangry woman. In any case, I just don't have patience for incompetence. Do your job and we'll get along fine. Security should've notified me immediately of suspected cheaters.

I gesture for Jean-Luc to come closer again and work to keep my voice even. "I need the names of the guards who noticed this." The incompetent ones.

He clears his throat and mumbles something unintelligible.

"Speak up," I order.

"Laurence and Albert." His voice cracks.

"Thank you." I swear I'm not a nightmare boss. I'm a perfectly reasonable man with a laid-back demeanor. No one can read my poker face. I must be cracking under the pressure of running this place single-handedly. That will be my next priority—hiring a pit boss to deal with the staff.

He shifts uneasily back and forth on the balls of his feet. "I should let you get to work."

I'm good at reading people—one of the keys to winning at poker, the other being my near photographic memory—and he has something on his mind that he's hesitant to say. More cheaters? I don't feel like guessing.

I keep my voice reasonable. "Jean-Luc, do you have anything else you need to tell me?"

He stares at my desk. "Nothing important."

I set my teeth, reaching for patience. "Anything *not* important you need to tell me?"

"I'd like the bartending job."

"You're quitting on me already?"

He wrings his hands together. "I'd still work for the casino. Just upstairs at the bar."

"Why?"

"Um, because it's fun. And there's tips."

I suppose it's not *fun* to work for me. This is my first time managing other people and I'm fucking it up. I'm tempted to say, *here's a tip, don't quit on the boss of the place one month into the job*. I get it, though. I'm twenty-five, not so much older than him. The bar scene is more appealing than cowering from your grumpy boss.

"Have you ever tended bar before?" I ask.

"Yes. Last summer in France."

"Find me a new assistant and the job is yours."

He claps, bouncing on the balls of his feet. "I have the perfect person. My aunt. She's a retired nursery school teacher. Very calm and patient."

Is that what he thinks I need? Someone who won't become agitated by me? Another insult to my newfound managerial skills. I must do better.

"Have her come in," I say. "I still want to interview her first. And then you train her Monday through Friday and work bar on the weekend."

"Thank you, sir!"

I don't bother to reply, irritated with the change in staff. It's been one month and already two people are leaving their posts—the bartender and my assistant. This is supposed to be a fun, rewarding place to work. Maybe I should organize some kind of morale booster like a poker tournament. Only that's what I'd like to do for fun. What would my staff like? I have no idea. I employed local islanders for the most part, and I'm beginning to realize I'm out of touch with them.

I sit at my desk with the pile of paperwork awaiting me, power on my laptop, and pull my phone from my trousers pocket and set it on the desk. The damn phone vibrated so much with calls and notifications on my short drive here that I turned it off. Where to start? I dash off an email to my brother Lucas, who's the CEO of all of Villroy's business ventures, and ask him to find me a pit boss. He's the one who has the staffing contacts.

Now what? Which task will make the most money? Marketing. That was supposed to be my brother Oscar's role before he fell head over ass in love with a princess from another kingdom, Polly. Now they're married and rule there as king and queen. Good for him, right? Except he's the reason I run this gig solo and had to find other less helpful investors. He pulled out his part of the money, which was the majority, and donated it to Polly's kingdom after a hurricane disaster. I'm happy for him. Really. No hard feelings. It's just hard to understand how he could give up so much just to be with her—his legacy here at the casino, his home, his last asset from his football days.

If you look big picture, relationships are a bad bet. He got lucky. I only play when the odds are in my favor. No woman has ever held my interest for long, and I always thought it kinder to say goodbye before the woman got too attached.

Okay, marketing. I can make this about numbers. Return on investment is the top priority. We opened in August when there was a full roster of guests for the spa and got off to a strong start from the spillover visitors. It's now mid-September and the spa guests are winding down, which means so are we. I need to find a way to draw people here for the casino itself. The spa sells cosmetics online to counter these lulls. We depend on in-person visits.

It's been a year since the spa and cosmetics line launched, and our economy is slowly improving, but we're not there yet. There's a lot of pressure on me to make this casino successful to ensure a stable, solid future. It's the first time I've ever had the opportunity to contribute to Villroy in a significant way, and I can't let my kingdom down.

I turn to my laptop, looking over the guest counts expected at the spa for the next six months. There's definitely going to be a lull. I dive in, considering various advertising revenues and possible returns on investment.

By the time I finish, I'm surprised to see it's noon. Crap. I didn't turn my phone on yet. I grab it and power it on, finding several voicemails and texts—work and personal. *Prioritize.* Which voicemail is most critical? I tap through them quickly and stop when I see my twin left me a message. Silvia always gets priority. We have a tight bond even though she lives in the US with her husband, Cade, now. I check the time. It's six a.m. in New York City. That's where she's working now as an editor at a children's publisher. She called just a few minutes ago. I press play on the voicemail.

"Hello, it's your favorite sister calling. Give me a call when you get a minute. I got in touch with Sara Travers last night, we went out for drinks, and something she said has me worried. Poker related, so I thought you could help. Bye!"

Sara Travers. A chill runs down my spine. How odd. Neither of us have heard from Sara since her parents died when she was thirteen. She didn't want to keep in touch when we were teens, and never returned our calls, emails, or texts. Silvia said it was because the two of us were reminders of Villroy, which was where Sara had happy summers with her parents, whom she'd never have again. It was rejection by association. The last time I saw Sara was at her parents' funeral.

I've thought about her, though, hoping she was doing well. Truth? I tried to connect with her as an adult, too, tracking her down through social media, but she never reciprocated. I finally accepted that she didn't want the connection. Still, some part of me never let her go.

Her birthday is August tenth—the day before the casino opened—and she turned twenty-five. That means we're both twenty-five, the age we vowed to marry. We made a pact. One of those silly things children do. We also vowed to play poker all night, every night as a married couple, unable to imagine anything more exciting a married couple could do. Ha! We may have only been twelve, but it felt intense at the time. She was my first kiss and it was *perfect.*

A pang of jealousy shoots through me. Sara got in touch with Silvia and not me? Sara adored me. She said I was her hero.

I press the button to return the call. "Hey, Sil, how're you doing?"

"Great! How's the casino business going?" She's a chirpy early bird to my night owl, which used to make for some tense mornings when we were kids as she chirped away to my irritated grunts.

"Casino business is going. What's this about Sara? How

did you get in touch? Did she contact you, or the other way around?" I grimace, hoping I don't sound jealous that Sara didn't get in touch with me too.

"I did a little digging and found her in Brooklyn. I just got to remembering all those good times we had together as kids, and then she just went away. I thought she'd be willing to see me since I'm practically a native New Yorker like her now."

I refrain from commenting. Silvia has only lived in New York for a few months, and her accent is still clearly from here. I'm told we speak a proper-sounding English with a slight French lilt. Villroy is just southwest of France, and many of the islanders are bilingual since Villroy was taken over by the British and then by the French before the rightful family, the Rourkes, took back control a couple of centuries ago.

I lean back in my seat. "So you called her and went out for drinks. What did she say that has you worried?"

"Actually, I just showed up on her doorstep. I wasn't sure if she'd try to avoid me. Luckily, she was home, and I guess she's in a better place now because she was happy to see me."

I should see her too. "What has you worried?"

"She said she's making good money now running a poker game in Brooklyn. She says it's legal. She just makes a lot in tips. Then I started thinking if she's making a lot in tips, then the pot must be really high. Who's attracted to a poker game like that? Really wealthy people, powerful people. Do you think it's Wall Street types or—"

"Organized crime."

"Exactly. I just kept picturing this poker game with high stakes, and then there's Sara running it alone, handling the money alone. Am I being paranoid?"

I consider this. Would Sara admit if there was any danger to what she was doing? I'm not sure. As kids, she loved a bet, loved a challenge, loved poker. This would be a natural fit for her. The only way to find out is to see the game in action and meet the players. No way am I sending Silvia into that situation. First, because it could be dangerous, and second, because she's not much of a poker player.

Cards on the table? I can't miss this chance to finally connect with Sara again. If she's open to seeing Silvia, she'll be open to seeing me. We're equal reminders of Villroy. Maybe she's moved past the grief tied to that reminder of her parents.

"Give me her address," I say.

"Are you coming for a visit? Yay! Bonus for me."

I find myself smiling. I just saw Silvia last month for the grand opening of the casino. "As if that wasn't your plan all along."

She laughs. "Yes, that was my nefarious plan. Play on your weakness for her."

"It wasn't a weakness. I liked her same as you."

Her voice is soft. "Sometimes I think it was harder on you than me when she cut us off."

I don't respond. It was tough, and obviously I never let her go, but that's the kind of thing Silvia would jump all over with her romantic sentimental ideals. For all I know, Sara and I won't even be compatible as adults, other than a shared love of poker. I don't have expectations. I just need to know that she's okay. And I'm curious about a person who was a big part of my childhood. Nothing romantic going on in the least.

"Okay, enough mushy talk from you," Silvia says in a teasing voice. "So you're going to check out her game?"

"Worth a look. I can't get away for long. I'll fly out on Monday since we're closed here on Mondays." Our private jet makes travel easy.

"The boss man."

"Not all glitz and glamour. My assistant cowers from me, and the staff can't get over my title to be straight with me."

"It's your voice. It comes out like a gruff growl when you're irritated. Personally, I find gruff, growly men endearing." She speaks away from the phone. "Yes, I mean you, love, and also my twin and my cousins." There's a kissy noise. Cade looks like a mountain man—six feet six, dirty blond hair left loose to his shoulders, with a full beard. He works for an outdoor recreation retail and services company as a financial analyst. He's gruff and outdoorsy. The near opposite of my sweet bookworm sister.

She gets back to me. "Cade overheard. Anyway, some people find that type of voice a wee bit intimidating. Add in the prince thing for locals who've only known you from afar and you've got uneasy staff."

"Nothing I can do about being a prince, and I can't help my voice when I'm irritated."

"Try to put some sweet into it like me."

"I'm sweet as pie," I growl, and she laughs.

"Make Emma take your place when you're gone," Silvia says. That's our older sister and investor in the casino. "She has a stake in it and should take more interest."

"I'll run it by her." I pause. "What's she like?" I mean Sara.

"She's the same but different. There's a hard toughness to her that she didn't used to have, but when she smiles, it's like old times. And Chloe is no longer the wild child. Sara says she's a very serious student. She just started at Columbia and plans to graduate in three years so she can go straight to Harvard Medical School. She wants to be a medical researcher and find a cure for cancer."

"Wow. That's...great." But concerning to hear the complete turnaround in Chloe's personality. She was never serious as a kid. Of course, the last time I saw her, she was only five. I never would've thought she'd be a serious student and a doctor. It seems there's a lot I don't know about Sara and her sister.

"I know, it's a little weird considering what a terror she was. I plan to visit her too. Okay, got to go. Text me when you get in town. Love you!"

"Love you too." I hang up and sit there for a moment, my mind replaying memories of Sara as a kid, teasing, playful, laughing. That summer when I rescued her and kissed her and made a solemn vow.

If Sara needs a hero, then, good news, I'm on my way. And if she doesn't, I have a good excuse—we're twenty-five, and we had a pact.

3

───────

Sara

I ring the bell of a Park Slope brownstone and tell myself to stay cool and confident. This is the hard part of my job. The morning after the poker game, I have to collect the debts from the losers before I can distribute the money to the winners. Sergei lost big last night. It's a balancing act with wealthy, powerful men. They don't want to lose face, don't want to be seen as the loser. I have to keep it light and fun.

A moment later, his housekeeper, Ms. Davies, a woman in her sixties with a short bob of gray hair, ushers me in. "Hello, Sara, he's in his office."

"Hello, Ms. Davies, and thank you."

I've been here before with his winnings, but never for such a big loss. I glance around. What am I worried about? He can afford it. Sergei lives alone in this prestigious historic neighborhood in a six-thousand-foot town house. It's a mansion, really. These places go for millions. Just look at this carved wood staircase original to the home, more than one hundred years old. That alone is probably worth more than my apartment. My heels click across herringbone parquet floors as I pass French doors leading into an elegant parlor.

I'm in a black and white striped short-sleeved blouse with a black pencil skirt and black pumps, going for the professional look. This is business. I turn to the open door of his office. Floor-to-ceiling bookcases filled with leather-bound books stretch the length of the wall on either side of the fireplace and above it. The room is well lit by two large windows on the far side of the room.

Sergei's back is to me as he stares at a photo on the fireplace mantel. He's a tall wiry man in his thirties with dark brown hair in a buzz cut that accentuates his sharp cheekbones.

Light and fun. "Morning, Sergei. Looks like a gorgeous day out."

He turns to me and smiles, his dark brown eyes glittering with shrewd intelligence. "Always good to see you, Sara, though I wish it were under better circumstances this morning." He has a slight Russian accent, which he's been working to lose with a private dialect coach. I know this because he asked me if I could detect his accent when we first met. Um, yeah, sure can.

I cross to him, and he gives me a once-over as I walk, taking in my outfit, lingering on my calves. My legs are bare. Guess he's a leg man.

I smile brightly. "I'm sure you'll be winning again in the very next game. You're the best player." One of the best.

"Let's talk," he says, indicating a pair of wooden chairs with blue cushioned seats in front of the fireplace. Not good. I don't want to talk. I want the money he owes me.

I take a seat and cross my legs. "What would you like to talk about?"

He angles his chair so he's facing me. "We haven't had much time just the two of us."

I paste on a smile. He's interested in me. No, thanks. "True, but I'm here now. I know it's not fun, but I do have a lot more stops to make, so if you could just give me what I came for, I'd be most appreciative."

His voice turns husky. "You're a beautiful woman. Have I ever told you that?"

"Thank you," I say evenly. "I appreciate that. I need to go;

others are expecting me. I could accept a check if that's easier."

His dark eyes are soft, his voice low. "Would you like to have dinner tonight?"

I look down and away, playing flattered. "Sergei, that's such a nice invitation." I meet his eyes, wait a beat as if I'm considering it, and then say in a regretful tone, "I need to decline. I don't date players. It would make the others suspicious if they thought I favored one player over another. I like to keep the game professional for all concerned."

This is true, but it's not just because he's a player and this is business for me. I don't do relationships, period. My sister is the only real tie I will keep until the day I die. I'd rather be alone than go through the pain of losing someone again. I don't need a therapist to tell me why. It is what it is. Most people are a bad bet anyway.

He leans his elbows on his knees, bringing his face down to my level, uncomfortably close. "No one would have to know. I wouldn't tell. You could keep a little secret, no?"

I push my chair back and stand. "I'm afraid not. I would like to keep our friendship as is."

He slowly stands and closes the distance, a predatory stealth to his movements. My heart pounds. I consider my options—knee in the balls, turn and run, scream. Wait. I have pepper spray in my purse.

He's so close I can feel his breath on my face. He tucks a lock of my hair behind my ear. "Such a pretty little thing."

I swallow hard, my hand sliding to the zipper of my purse. "I heard Vic Sobol has been asking about our game. He's that—"

He stills. "I know who he is. He runs that hedge fund. You can get him?"

"I'm meeting with him later. I can get him from curious to itching to play. Definitely." This is a total bluff. I've been putting out feelers for Vic and haven't heard back. I'll worry about that later.

His eyes narrow. "You play us all, don't you?"

My hand dives into my purse, frantically searching for the

pepper spray. "My job is to run a fair game with the best players. Like you." I've got it, my finger on the nozzle. I debate whipping out the pepper spray. If I do it prematurely, I've cut this player forever. He was one of the first players in my game when it was only five men, and he's brought some great players with him. We've got ten men now with loads to gamble. They may all take his side, leaving me without a decent game. "You understand this is my job, right? Run the game; keep everyone even. I'm putting my little sister through college. I'm all she has. We're orphans." I ignore the sharp jab of pain over my parents and remain focused on the task at hand.

He turns to his desk across the room, and I nearly collapse with relief, releasing my hold on the pepper spray. I watch as he pulls open a drawer and produces a checkbook.

"I lost my mother young," he says as he writes out a check. He hands it to me. "Your sister is lucky to have you."

I take the check, glance at the amount to be sure he didn't stiff me, and tuck it into my purse. "Thank you. I'll see you Tuesday night with the new fish." Fish means a bad player, which is a lot of fun for skilled players like him to play with. I'm implying the hedge fund guy will be bad at poker, though we both know he's not. Keeping it light and fun.

He shakes his head. "That would be ideal. Not likely that Vic will be a fish."

I back toward the door. "I value our friendship greatly, Sergei. And I'm a bad bet anyway. I don't do relationships."

He smirks. "Who said anything about a relationship?"

I shake my finger at him. "I don't do that with my players either. Have a good day!"

And then I'm gone, walking at a brisk pace out of what I'm calling a successful collection visit. Only four more to go. Then I get to do the fun part, bringing the money to the winners. Everyone loves those visits. I'm like Robin Hood, except I take from the rich and make the rich richer. Maybe I'm more like a fairy godmother. All I know is I fucking love this job.

By the time I get home to my studio apartment in a not-so-nice neighborhood of Brooklyn, far from the Park Slope richies, I'm flying high. All of my players are paid, everyone's eager for Tuesday, and the world is a golden place. I toss my purse on my dark green futon and go to the galley kitchen, pulling the safe from the oven. My favorite pastime, counting my money. It's not like I'm Miss Greedy. I really am putting my sister through college and hopefully medical school too. Our parents died in an accident when I was thirteen. My chest aches, and I realize I'm holding my breath. I remind myself to breathe normally as the memory washes over me. *Breathe in, breathe out. Panic attacks do not control me anymore.*

They'd gone out for a date night, walking to a restaurant not far from our Manhattan apartment. They were trying to work things out after many heated arguments over my dad wanting to quit his job in favor of starting a new business as a consultant. A drunk truck driver veered off the road and plowed into them on the sidewalk. I like to think they were trying to make peace and not fighting in their last moments.

I grew up overnight. Wrenched from my secure idyllic life into the harsh reality that I was alone in the world. Of course, I had Chloe. She was only six, a baby, and I stepped up to be the mom she missed out on. We moved to Brooklyn to live with our uncle Rob in a two-bedroom apartment in a nice neighborhood. It wasn't too bad. He was a nice guy, but flaky. I became the adult in that household, cooking, cleaning, and taking care of Chloe. She went from a wild child to mute overnight. It took three months to get her speaking again, and she never did go back to her energetic carefree self. She became serious and withdrawn, even with counseling. Who could blame her? It was a dark time.

When I was sixteen, Uncle Rob lost his job and moved to Nashville to make it big with his new girlfriend, leaving us behind. Then I really was the adult in charge. He sent some money for the rent, and I covered the rest working as a waitress. I thought he'd come to his senses, but he never returned. Chloe and I took stock and decided we needed a cheaper apartment, this tiny place, and our best bet was to live extremely frugally until I was eighteen and could get a higher-paying job. Finally, I graduated high school and got a job as an office manager, working there days and waitressing at night. Chloe worked her ass off at school, deciding college would be her springboard to a better life. But then she found she really liked school. She was good at it. Now her aspirations are both for financial security and to make a difference in the world. I'm so proud of her.

As for me, I've been a player in local poker games for years before it dawned on me I could make a lot more by running my own game. Ever since I got this game going this summer, all of my money worries vanished. I quit both my jobs *and* I paid Chloe's first tuition bill in August. It's looking fantastic for the January bill. I don't want her to leave college in deep debt, especially knowing the cost of medical school. Last night I pulled in fifty thousand in tips. The pot keeps getting higher and higher with the players I'm attracting— wealthy Russians—and I make sure everyone leaves the game feeling like they're the king. Maybe Chloe won't have to work so hard to finish college in three years. I want her to enjoy her time in college, not rush through it. Though she swears she's not doing undergrad in three years for financial reasons. She claims she just can't wait to get to medical school. Knowing Chloe, it's probably both. Now that she's eighteen, she has some perspective on what I did for her, trying to be the mom she missed out on, and wants to give back to me. Silly girl. That's not how the little-sister gig works.

I take the safe to my futon and sit with it on my lap, doing the combination and opening it. Stacks of hundred-dollar bills greet me with their reassuring presence. I should probably put these in a bank, but I fear looking suspicious showing up with so much cash. They might think I robbed a convenience store or something. At this point, I could even prepay next year's tuition and still have some left over for rent.

I should upgrade to a one-bedroom apartment. This one is so small—one room with my futon sofa that pulls out to a queen-sized bed, a galley kitchen, and a separate tiny bathroom. Hard to believe until recently I shared this small space with Chloe. She's not far, in a dorm at Columbia in the city, but I miss her terribly.

I pull out the stacks of bills, counting them and then spreading them out on the coffee table to make them look like even more. I smile and gather them up, carefully sliding them back in the safe. Oops. I accidentally flipped over my lucky dragon cards—a pair of red twos. I carefully place them facedown in the very back. They're the only thing I kept from before my life turned upside down. They remind me of a simpler time when I believed a sweet boy with hazel eyes was my hero.

I'm sure Adrian has moved on. I was just the summer visitor. He's a prince moving in elite circles. He tried to get in touch over the years, but I just wasn't ready to look back to my time on Villroy. My parents were like a honeymooning couple in our rented summer cottage there. It was too heartbreaking to revisit those memories with a reality that didn't include them. I needed to stay strong for Chloe. Eventually, Adrian stopped reaching out.

I close and lock my safe. Maybe I should ask Silvia for his number. I'm in a better place now. I saw Silvia here in Brooklyn and that went well. No expectations or anything. Just for old times' sake.

Adrian

I stare out the window of the rented Mercedes, looking for numbers on the buildings we pass. Looks like it's just up ahead. I tell the driver where to stop, and my guard, Jack, steps out with me a few moments later. He's thirty with a blond buzz cut, tall and wide with a hard expression that lets everyone know not to try anything on his watch. After all my time sparring with the palace guards, I could defend myself, but I'm required to have a guard as part of the royal family. I chose Jack because he always presents a challenge when we spar. In any case, it's smart to have someone looking over my shoulder for the rare times when there's an overzealous crowd.

It's Monday afternoon New York time, and I'm standing in front of a run-down concrete and glass building in a questionable neighborhood in Brooklyn. It doesn't look like Sara's swimming in money like Silvia said. I hope she's home. I'll sit on the front steps until she shows up if I have to. It's warmer than I thought it would be for mid-September. I undo my cuffs and roll up my shirtsleeves. Then I hesitate, staring at the intercom button with her name on it—Travers.

I blow out a breath. Some part of me isn't sure I'll get the warm reception my sister got. Silvia and Sara were best friends in that tight way girls can be. I was an add-on to their friendship until that last summer when Sara and I got closer. I was her hero.

I shake my head at myself. The heroic efforts of a twelve-year-old boy. She's probably forgotten all about it with the way things changed so drastically for her. I'm here to make sure she's not in any danger with her poker game. That's it.

Okay, I'm dying to see what she looks like all grown up in person. Her pic on social media was taken from a distance, and she wore a baseball cap with sunglasses.

I press the intercom.

A female voice carries through. "Yeah?"

I clear my throat. "Sara?"

"Who wants to know?" Her voice sounds tough just like Silvia said.

"It's Adrian Rourke. Silvia gave me your address. I was in town and thought I'd stop by."

Silence.

Shit. Am I getting the brush-off? Silvia showed up unannounced with no problem.

A moment later, the door opens and she's standing right in front of me—Sara Travers all grown up.

My mouth goes dry. She's even more beautiful than I remember. Her blond hair is down to her shoulders in a straight silky cascade; her thick lashes frame green eyes, her skin creamy. Her body is all woman, curvy and toned, in a faded pink T-shirt with white denim cut-off shorts, really short shorts, shapely legs, bare feet. Every nerve ending goes on high alert, my pulse thrumming through my veins. Straight-up lust. Guess that attraction we flirted with at twelve didn't go away. Now I actually know what to do about it.

I force my gaze back to her face. The seven freckles across her cute nose are still there. My lucky number. The freckles are muted, probably with makeup, but they're there. She's still my Sara from the best summers of my life. I didn't realize just how much I missed her until this very moment.

My voice comes out hoarse. "Sara."

Her green eyes are wide, staring at me. "Adrian?"

I smile. "The one and only."

Her gaze searches my features, her voice soft. "I can't believe you're here. You look so different."

"All grown up. You look different, too, in a good way. How are you?"

She turns inside, gesturing for me to follow. "Come in."

I follow her upstairs, my guard trailing me, and she opens the door to a tiny apartment. I turn back to Jack. "You can wait outside."

"I need to take a look around, Your Highness," Jack says.

"Is it okay?" I ask Sara.

She gestures him in. "Sure. Not much to see."

Jack goes in and steps out a minute later. "All clear, sir."

"Thanks," I say.

"I'll be outside, sir," he says.

I nod at Jack and follow Sara into a one-room apartment. It's clean but sparse—an old green futon, a beat-up wooden coffee table, and a small black end table with a lamp. Tiny galley kitchen. Maybe Sara's version of "good money" from poker game tips is a lot less than Silvia's version of good money. I don't know what Sara's used to since her parents died. They used to be well off, I think. At least enough to live in Manhattan and spend summers on Villroy, though her father never stayed the whole summer. He did something in finance. Her mother was headmaster at a private school, where Sara went for free, so her mother had summers off.

I study her face for a moment, trying to see the tough hardness Silvia mentioned. She sounded tough on the intercom, but she doesn't look tough to me, more like an assured competency. Like she knows exactly who she is and what she wants to do. She has a much more serious expression than when she was a kid, but that's to be expected, especially when she basically had to grow up overnight with the death of her parents. As the older sister by seven years, I'm sure she looked after little Chloe too. I like this look on her. I appreciate competent people.

She turns to the small refrigerator, opens the door, and bends down to look inside. "Can I get you anything to eat or drink?"

My gaze lands on her heart-shaped ass in short shorts, and my skin prickles with awareness, my hands itching to touch. I tear my gaze away, trailing down her smooth toned legs. Raw desire surges through me. *Look away, look away.* I remind myself I'm only in town for a few days. I need to fly home Thursday to be at the casino for the busy weekend time. I could never treat Sara like a casual fling, which means just friends. My gaze drifts up her legs to her sweet ass. *Thong? Bikini underwear? Lace or cotton?* My trousers get tight. Fuck.

She turns, and I jerk my head up to meet her eyes. She gives me an apologetic smile. "Maybe we should go out. I don't have anything but condiments, old takeout, and wilted lettuce. I wasn't expecting company."

"Is it an imposition, me showing up here? Silvia said she just showed up, so…"

She plants her hands on her hips in a stance I remember well. "The Rourke twins within days of each other. So crazy. I just can't believe you're really here. So you just got in town?"

She was my first stop after the airport. *Sorry, sis!* "Got in today. Let's go. Drinks on me."

"Sure."

Her cheeks flush pink as she reaches behind me to grab

her purse from the futon. I love that her skin gives her away —getting closer to me made her pink up. Maybe this lust goes both ways.

"I guess Silvia told you about our visit?" she asks, tucking the strap of her purse over her shoulder.

"She mentioned it. I was coming to visit her anyway so thought I'd stop by and say hello." I smile and say warmly, "Hello."

"Hello." Her voice is breathy. She stares at my lips for a moment, then my jaw—I've let it get scruffy—her gaze dropping to my shoulder and then my exposed forearm. Her cheeks *and* neck are flushed pink now. The attraction is definitely mutual. I'm secretly pleased, even though I'm not going to do anything about it.

I can't help myself. "Like what you see?"

Her hand flutters in the air, her cheeks flaming bright pink. Embarrassed this time. "Sorry." She rushes out the door.

I follow her out and watch her lock it behind us. I keep it light. "I don't mind you ogling me," I say as we head downstairs. "I'm shockingly manly, and you're trying to reconcile it with how you last saw me."

She bursts out laughing, and my chest warms. "True. I may remember you prepuberty."

"I was in the throes of it last time I saw you."

She stops on the sidewalk outside. "I'll take you to the same place I took Silvia. It's a nice restaurant with a bar, where your guard won't be looked at with suspicion."

"Drive or walk?"

"We can walk. It's a nice night."

"Lead the way."

We head down the street at a brisk pace. Sara has that New Yorker stride, purposeful and fast, like there's no time to waste. My guard trails behind us.

"Silvia's exactly the same," she says. "Still a bookworm. She even looks the same just taller." She glances up at me. "I don't mean to stare at you. I'm just trying to reconcile this look with how you were."

"Guess it's going to take some time to get over the shock

of me in all my manly glory." I pound my chest with a fist in a Neanderthal display.

She doesn't laugh. Instead, she tucks her hair behind her ears, pink dotting her cheeks as she looks straight ahead. "It is a bit of a shock. So what've you been up to lately?"

"Should I give you the rundown since we last spoke?"

"Sure. Tell me about the past thirteen years."

"Graduated from Cambridge, where I studied mathematics with a concentration in statistics and probability. I immediately put my degree to use as a stellar poker player. Important work, I know. Now I run a casino on Villroy and watch other people lose at poker."

She nods. "Sounds perfect for you. How's the casino business?"

"Well, it's only been a month, but we got off to a flying start. It helps that we get the overflow of clients from the day spa next door, and they're really busy in the summer. Now I just have to figure out how to keep visitors up, and how to be a little sweeter."

She looks up at me quizzically. "Sweeter?"

"Silvia says I need to put more sweet in my voice." I lift one shoulder. "Just because my assistant cowers from me and staff are afraid to come to me with problems."

Her brows draw together. "Bad advice. The boss can't be sweet. It's good that they fear you."

"It's not like they're terrified. They're just intimidated by my title and the fact that I have no patience for incompetency."

"And you shouldn't tolerate incompetency. They can't do the work—" she hitches a thumb and lets out a sharp whistle "—so long! Now the customers, that's another story. It's all light and fun for them."

"Is that how you run your poker game?"

She stiffens. "Silvia told you about that?"

"Yes, she thought I might like to play while I was in town. You have room at the table tomorrow? She said you play Tuesdays."

"No room, sorry. We've got our ten."

"How about I just watch? I could rotate in if someone wants to take a break or leaves early. It happens."

"I'll let you know."

My senses go on full alert. She's being cagey, not even letting me watch. "You play twice a week, right? When's the next game after that?"

"How's the rest of your family? I heard Gabriel is king now. Crap. Sorry." She winces. "I'm sorry about your dad."

"Thanks. My family is doing well. Gabriel is doing a fantastic job as leader, along with his wife. They're taking Villroy into the next century while still holding on to our history and traditions. It was a genius move to transition the commercial fishing industry to cosmetics manufacturing using stuff from the sea. Fish oil, algae, and the like."

"That's great to hear. Silvia told me a bit about it. She sounded really proud of her part in helping with research for the cosmetics and the spa."

"It's been a family venture, everyone involved. I'm proud of what we've accomplished too."

We walk in silence for a few moments. It's comfortable like we're walking along the beach again, some part of us remembering each other despite all the time that's passed. I want to know more about her game, her life, basically everything, but there's one thing I'm dying to know most of all.

"Do you remember our pact?" I ask with a smile.

Her expression goes blank. "Pact? We had a pact?"

"You don't remember?" She must. It was an intense moment. At least for me. "We said we'd meet up again when we were twenty-five and get married."

"I never said that."

"Yes, you did. It wasn't *my* idea. I was just angling for a kiss that summer."

She laughs a little. "Sounds like the silly fantasy of a silly girl."

"We are twenty-five now."

Her jaw drops. "Are you serious? You want to marry me because of a pact we made as kids? You barely know me."

I can't help my laugh. "You should see your face. Horror show! Married to me. Although…" I flex a bicep.

"Stop," she says on a laugh.

I elbow her. "We did make a solemn vow on my dragon cards. The plan was to play poker all night, every night as a married couple. I was pretty excited about that part."

She shakes her head, smiling. "You remember a lot from when we were kids."

I get serious. "I never forgot you, Sara. I always hoped you were doing okay. I really wanted to keep in touch."

Her green eyes go soft, and she looks away. "I'm sorry I didn't. Life was really rough for a long time, but I'm in a good place now."

"Where did you go? Who took care of you?"

"Chloe and I moved to Brooklyn with my uncle Rob. My mother's younger brother. No worries. Nice guy." Her voice catches, and she points up ahead. "Ooh. This place has the best pizza in town."

That's why I couldn't find her number or address listed. The apartment must've been under her mother's maiden name since it was her mother's younger brother. I was looking for Travers.

I focus back on her. "You want pizza?"

"No. Just pointing out the sights since you're new in town."

I let her give me the tour, which is mostly places she likes to eat as well as the best vintage clothing shops. I know when to drop a touchy subject. I'm enjoying getting to know her again. Now all I need is an invite to her game.

I'm betting I'll have it by the end of the night.

4

Sara

I'm in shock. Like I'm having an out-of-body experience sitting at this bar with Adrian, my brain slowly trying to keep up. It's like I conjured him from my thoughts. My lucky dragon cards flip up, I think of Adrian and getting in touch, and suddenly he's on my doorstep!

Adrian morphed from a sweet cute boy to a hot-as-fuck man. It's really messing with my head. He's got the same thick dark brown hair, same warm hazel eyes, but the rest! Jesus. My hormones are rioting. I pray he hasn't noticed. It feels like I'm blushing head to toe. He's six feet at least, wide shoulders, muscular and fit. There's *scruff* on his square jaw. Dark, delicious scruff. His lips are sensual, kissing lips. And his voice! So deep and sexy. He smells like spice and sex. I mean, spice and man.

I'm *not* going to hook up with him. He was a good friend of mine before my life split into a sharp before and after. I could never treat him like a hookup, and I'm not up for a relationship. Too risky, too painful when he leaves, and I know he will. He's tied to the casino in Villroy, a place I never want to see again, and I'm tied here to Chloe. She needs me. I'm her legal guardian and the only mother she remembers. Not to mention this fantastic game I've got going here, which will pay my sister's tuition for undergrad and medical school. I can't leave the best job I've ever had.

I've cyberstalked him over the years—a dirty secret I've never told anyone about, not even my sister. He was my weakness, my only soft spot, a fantasy that helped me through tough times. My hero, my prince, who would one day come for me. I bluffed earlier, too embarrassed to admit I remembered the pact. Some secret part of me fantasized it would come true and it would be like a romantic dream—my sweet prince and I would live happily ever after playing poker in a house big enough to include my sister. I always fantasized we'd get a house just outside the city, with a yard for our kids and dog. Such a simple normal fantasy to live in the burbs that I never believed would come true. He belongs in Villroy, that's his kingdom, and I belong here. I never thought I'd see Adrian again after I didn't respond to his initial attempts to get in touch. Yet, by some miracle, here he is. It's like my fantasy came true.

What girl doesn't dream of marrying a prince and becoming a princess? I never cared about the princess part. I dreamed of marrying a prince who was my equal in poker, so we could play together night and day. I barely understood what sex was back then. All I knew was it involved naked time, which sounded embarrassing.

It's so weird how much seeing him in person is affecting me. I knew what he looked like from pictures on the internet. He's got powerful pheromones or testosterone, I don't know, but I'm ridiculously flustered by it. I knew he went to Cambridge just like he dreamed of, I was happy to see him lending his name to charitable causes, and I knew he owned the casino and ran it. I frequently saw him in the company of beautiful women and never the same woman. No judgment here. He's a gorgeous prince in his twenties, which means he doesn't need to settle down. And me? I haven't been with a man in a long while. Maybe six months? Oh, shit. It's been nine months. I got lonely over New Year's and Chloe was sleeping over at a friend's house, so I brought a guy home from a bar. Never saw him again, which was fine with me.

So now what? We just finished drinks. Adrian had a beer. I had a shot of tequila, which did nothing to calm me. I know him but don't know him, and my brain can't reconcile my memories with whoever he is today. It must be the hormones standing in the way. I need to treat him just like I did his sister—friendly, and then *so long, let's keep in touch.*

He leans close, his deep voice rumbling in my ear, and I suppress a shiver. "You want to shift to a table and get some dinner?"

Do I want to spend more time with him?

He grins, his hazel eyes sparkling with good humor. "You did say you only had wilted lettuce at home. How about some fresh lettuce? Maybe a steak to go with it?"

I laugh. "Fresh lettuce with steak sounds good." We are at a fantastic steakhouse. "I wasn't angling to get a steak dinner. I just like the laid-back vibe of the bar here."

"Never thought you were."

He signals to a waitress, who rushes over to him. She's caught in the Adrian testosterone force field, or maybe she recognizes him. The last bachelor prince of Villroy. His older brothers are all married now.

I glance over at him, and he gives me a small smile that warms me so much I have to look away. I'm not used to this intensity of feeling. Adrian was my first kiss, and I'm so glad. It was *perfection.* My kisses after him were sloppy, wet, too soft, too hard. Horribly imperfect. And when I got older, when I was pickier about who I kissed, they were just there. The gateway to the main event. I enjoy sex, but once it's done, I'm done.

A few minutes later, we're shown to a square dark wood table for two in a private back corner. His guard hovers near the entrance to the space.

Adrian pulls out my chair for me and tucks it in as I sit. I remember this, the gentleman manners. They teach that up at the palace. Even at twelve, he would open doors for us girls. I never gave much thought to him being a prince until we got older. When we met at eight years old, he was just the annoying sidekick to my awesome new friend Silvia. I was so thrilled to find her on the beach one day because Chloe was a one-year-old bore. In fact, that first summer I thought Adrian was gross because he ran around the beach with sand stuck to him and never cared enough to wash it off. He always got sand all over our towels and chairs. Plus, he stuffed sandwiches in his mouth and chewed with big chipmunk cheeks. *Boys! Eww!* How things change.

I need to keep this thing with Adrian light. No expectations, just a friendly visit. It was easier with Silvia. She happily chattered on about the books she's working on for the children's publisher, where she works. Adrian is more reserved, which makes me want to fill the silence, but I have to be careful not to share too much. I can't let myself get close enough to be hurt when he leaves.

"How long are you in town for?" I ask once he takes his seat across from me.

"Until Thursday," he says. "The weekend is busy for the casino."

"Ah, quick visit. Too bad. My game runs Tuesdays and Thursdays, so you'll just miss the second game."

"I'll be there tomorrow, then." He leans across the table. "I'll play poorly, and they'll be thrilled to see the chips piling up."

I flush with heat just because he leaned close. He's just so impossibly sexy. *Cool it!* I busy myself putting my napkin in my lap. "The guys don't like people they don't know."

"You can vouch for me. Besides, at least one of them must have heard of me. My family's been getting a lot of press lately between the day spa and my casino." He taps his chest with both hands. "I'm a prince, you know."

I roll my eyes. "Yes, I know. I just don't think—"

"Bet you're too chicken to invite me to your game."

My hackles rise. "I'm not chicken." Then I realize what he's done, appealing to my inner twelve-year-old. "Nice try."

He smirks.

The waitress arrives, telling us about the specials and asking what we'd like to drink.

"You want to share a bottle of wine?" he asks.

Oh boy. That would be bad. I can be very loosey-goosey when I drink too much. "I'll stick to water. Get whatever you want."

"We'll both have water," he says.

Once she leaves, Adrian studies me. Maybe he also finds it strange to see me as a full-grown woman. I doubt he's seen any pictures of me on the internet over the years except for the distant fuzzy profile pic I posted on social media when I set it up years ago. This really is his first time seeing me.

He places his hand facedown on the table in front of me. "Okay, cards on the table. Silvia's worried about your game, and I told her I'd check it out. I'm not going to ruin it or end it. I'm just going to check it out and tell Silvia there's nothing to worry about."

I let out a breath. I'm glad he's being straightforward with me, so I do the same. "There *is* nothing to worry about. You can tell her that right away."

"I need to see for myself."

I speak through my teeth. "I appreciate your concern, but you don't get to play overprotective he-man friend here. You don't know me well enough to have any authority over me." I lift a finger. "*Not* that I'd ever let you have authority over me. I've been taking care of myself just fine for years, so chill. Everything's great."

He chuckles. "He-man friend. That's a new one."

I bite back a smile. "Glad you like it."

"I'm very chill." He gives me a charming smile, his eyes twinkling. "Come on, there's always room at a game for me. People know my rep as a card shark. The good players want to say they bested me. If you have any decent players, I'll let them win."

"You're willing to lose? You *hate* to lose. You're as competitive as I am."

His hazel eyes are direct, intent on mine. "I've learned sometimes other things are more important."

I swallow hard. Does he mean *I'm* more important? It almost feels like he cares about me, but how could he after all these years? "Silvia's being a pain in the ass about it, isn't she?"

He lifts one shoulder. "You know Silvia."

I used to. I kind of still do. She's still the same old Silvia—sweet and warm. The girl next door, except she's a princess. That never came between us, either, because she never made a big deal out of being a princess. She always seemed a little embarrassed by her guard and her maid, Marie, who doubled as a nanny and had been with her and Adrian since they were born.

"What's the buy-in?" he asks.

"Table's full. I've got my ten players."

"Humor me and answer the question. There's a steak dinner in it for you."

I consider if I want to answer. I'm sure he has the money to join the game. I could always work him in as an alternate. I'm just not sure I want him there. Everyone knows each other, and there's a good rapport going. Sergei is expecting me to come through with Vic, the hedge fund manager, though I still haven't heard back from him. Actually, Adrian might be even better than Vic—a celebrity with deep pockets —and if he plays poorly on purpose, they'll be thrilled to beat him. But then I'm basically asking him to make a giant donation to the cause just to appease his sister's unfounded worries.

"Tell Silvia not to worry, okay?" I say and pick up the menu.

"How much?" he demands in a growl that jolts me into dropping the menu as excitement shoots through me.

That growly commanding voice does it for me. It's sexy as fuck, but it's also coming from someone I know is a good person. My personal kryptonite—alpha and tender, an extremely rare combination I've only read about in romance novels, which I will *never* admit to reading secretly on my phone. I have a tough New Yorker rep to protect.

I lick my lips. "Fifty K."

He blows out a breath. "You're telling me you've got a half mil on the table before the first cards are dealt?"

"Shh."

He leans close, his voice low. "Do you take a percent?"

"No." A rake, taking a percent, would make it illegal. Everything is completely kosher—I pay my taxes as an event planner, which I am. No rake, no drugs, just vodka and men looking for the adrenaline rush of the game.

His sharp eyes study me, and it feels like he's searching my soul for the truth about me. Truth? I don't let anyone see inside. It's all I can do not to fidget in my seat.

Finally, he says, "Tips must be great."

"Better than waitressing." And my office manager job combined, I add silently.

"Then why are you living in a studio apartment?"

"It's convenient."

"Where do you play?"

I pick up the menu and study it, hoping he'll take the hint. I don't want to answer any more questions. He doesn't take the hint *at all*. I can practically feel his eyes boring into the menu between us, and there's a palpable tension vibrating in the air. Alpha doesn't just mean sexy time, it means *all* the time. Clearly he's got the demanding, assertive, and protector parts down pat, but I don't need someone watching over me.

"Are you the only woman there?" he asks.

I keep studying the menu.

He snatches the menu from my hands. "Stop hiding behind the menu and answer me."

My stomach flutters. Fuck. I do *not* want to be turned on by Adrian Rourke. He's the one person who could easily get under my skin, and I can't risk the pain of letting him in close. He'll leave. Everyone leaves.

I avoid his eyes and take a deep breath, reaching for calm. He's tied to Villroy, and he's leaving on Thursday. I can handle this. He's just an old friend looking out for me because that's what he does. He has a hero complex. Oh, I feel so much better now. That's what this is. I called him a hero once, and now he thinks he has to play hero for me.

I meet his eyes. "Sometimes a few of the guys bring their

latest girlfriend, so I'm not always the only woman. I have a dealer I can depend on. I'm just the organizer."

"Organize me in," he orders.

Alpha. Hero. Why do I like that so much? I take care of myself.

I lean forward. "Why do you care what I do?"

He leans close, and my breath catches. "Why do you think?"

I gulp and lean back. "I have no idea. We barely know each other."

"Okay, let's get to know each other again." He lifts a hand. "Ask me anything, and then I'll ask you what I want to know, until we've reached friendship level again and then…" His voice drops to a fierce low tone that makes me go damp between the legs. "You tell me what the hell you're up to with this game that you won't even let me watch."

"I love your voice," I blurt. He did *not* sound like this at twelve.

He straightens. "You do?"

I nod.

He lifts a brow. "This is the voice that makes me a bad manager."

"I'm sure it's their issue, not yours."

He studies me for a long moment. "You should go back with me to Villroy to check out the casino. I'd love your opinion on it. I'll wait until after your game on Thursday, and you can take the jet with me. I'll have you back in time for your Tuesday game."

The jet. Maybe one day I'll be casually saying stuff like that. With the right people at my game, it's a possibility. But Villroy is a no-go. I don't want to be pulled under by grief again, don't want to chance losing control to panic attacks. I'm in a good place now. "Tempting, but I have to deal with the money the next day."

"What do you mean?"

I wave a hand airily. "You know, pay everyone up. Collect from the losers and give to the winners."

His eyes narrow. "You do that."

"Yes."

"By yourself."

I square my shoulders. "Well, yeah. It's my game. I'm not going to send someone else out. They might take a cut."

He slaps a palm on the table. "That's it. I'm going with you to the game, and the next day too. Are you financing these games yourself?"

"It's a risk, I know, but so far it's worked out."

"And what if they don't pay up the next day?"

"They always do."

His eyes bore into mine, his jaw set tight. "And, if they don't, you're on the hook to pay up the winners."

I meet his eyes and say evenly, "It's fine."

"It is *not* fine," he growls.

My nipples harden to points, my breasts aching and full. It's his voice, and also he sounds like he really cares about me. I don't know why he cares after all this time, but it's clear he's looking out for me. *My hero.*

"Whatever," I say with a casualness I'm far from feeling. "You can go to the game as an alternate and watch me do my job, but I'm sure you'll be bored out of your mind. It's all very mundane business."

"Great," he says in a cheerful voice that doesn't make me throb. *Much better.*

Of course, now I have to risk the guys revolting against an unknown. I'd better text everyone and talk Adrian up ahead of time. Prince of Villroy should do it. We don't have any celebrities at our game. Just wealthy business guys. I don't know what business they're all in, and I don't need to know. I screened them ahead of time to be sure no one was involved with drugs, human trafficking, or shit like that. My job is simply to make it fun for everyone—great food, great drink, quality chips and cards, nice table. This isn't the kind of game most guys have in the basement of some crap apartment building. I'm the key to making it great. I've even got a waiting list of players now, but I'm picky, looking for just the right people.

The rest of dinner goes smoothly. Adrian drops the poker

game inquisition and tells me all about his casino and the challenges of running it. His big concern is being a good manager, but guess what? Just the fact that he gives a shit about being a good manager automatically makes him one in my book. In my experience, most bosses don't care. He just needs to have a good team of people in place.

"I'm sure things will smooth out soon," I tell him. "You've just opened. Give it time for everyone to settle in and know their place."

He rubs the back of his neck, smiling. "I always knew you were smart."

I smile. "That's a huge compliment coming from you."

"Why is that?"

"Because you graduated with honors from Cambridge."

He cocks his head. "I didn't tell you I graduated with honors. Sara Travers, have you been cyberstalking me?"

I fight back a blush and work for my perfect poker face. "Silvia mentioned it."

"Ah. Did you go to university?"

I rub my finger back and forth on the edge of the table. "No. I needed to work. Money was tight." I lift my chin, pasting on a smile. "My goal was always to get Chloe through college, and she's doing fantastic. She got into Columbia."

"I'm glad to hear it. Do you ever think of going back?"

"What's the point? I'm doing great. Besides, I still have to get Chloe through medical school too. I'm not letting her graduate with heavy debt."

The waitress arrives with the check.

"My treat," I tell him, wanting him to know I'm doing great now and not trying to mooch a meal. I pick up the check, and he snatches it out of my hands.

"You can get the next dinner," he says, pulling out his wallet.

Next dinner? "But you're leaving on Thursday," I blurt.

"It's Monday. Maybe you'll need to eat again between now and then." He winks and—

I *melt.*

There's no other word for it. Warmth floods me and I

soften, all of my muscles relaxing. Adrian is something special—smart, warm, a really good person. I knew it when I was a kid, and I'm beginning to know it again. Throw in his sexy good looks, and he is temptation personified. I can't let myself get sucked in, can't let myself risk the pain of getting close to someone who lives an ocean away.

He walks me home, and the conversation is easy as he tells me about the latest with his family. There's been some crazy stuff going on up there at the palace. I knew about some of it, like the furry wedding (people in stuffed-animal suits) that was hilariously covered in detail in two bridal magazines and all over the internet, as well as his sister Emma running away from her own wedding. The bridal competition for his oldest brother Gabriel's hand was news though.

"So that's how he ended up marrying a commoner," I say. "That made headlines."

He nods. "It was a big deal with Gabriel being the heir to the throne, but my parents agreed to it because they didn't want another replay of what happened with my uncle. Did I ever tell you that story? How my father's older brother fell in love with a girl from Brooklyn and abdicated the throne to marry her?"

I shake my head.

He looks around. "I should look them up too while I'm here. That was the first time a royal married a commoner in our kingdom's history. It was a *huge* scandal. My uncle was exiled from Villroy forever, as well as his family. Silvia got in touch with my cousins here in Brooklyn since she's been in the US so long. I have six cousins I've never met."

"Wow. Who knew commoners were such a big deal."

"Only for the heirs to the throne. Us lower-down royals can marry as we please. My brother Phillip married an American too, a friend of Gabriel's wife. Emma married a British rock star, Jackson Walker."

"Go, Emma! Jackson is *fi-i-ne*." I clear my throat at his hard look. "I mean, if you're into that whole British bad-boy thing. Barf, right? Give me a straitlaced goody-goody any day."

"Goody-goody," he echoes.

"Math nerds preferred," I quip and then slap a hand over my mouth. "I did *not* mean you."

"Uh-huh."

"You're the exception to the rule. The one math guy who *isn't* a nerd."

He lifts a palm. "Moving on."

Oops! I offended him accidentally. "You're very manly in a nonnerdy way," I assure him and quickly move to another topic. "Definitely look up your cousins, uncle, and aunt while you're here. That's so sad that you have this whole family you've never met."

"Not exactly sad. I mean, I never met them, so I never knew what I was missing. Silvia says my cousins are gruff and growly."

"Ooh, I like gruff and growly."

"Do you now?" he growls in a deep voice.

A hot shiver races through me, my belly quivering. Ah, hell. Now he knows how to get to me. I swallow hard as he lifts my arm, murmuring, "Goose bumps." He stills, stroking a finger down my forearm, and those goose bumps aren't going anywhere. He lifts heated eyes to mine. "Interesting."

Our eyes lock for a long hypnotic moment. My breath stalls, my pulse scrambling. The attraction crackles in the air between us. This is not one-sided. Self-preservation kicks in, and I pull my arm free from his grip, resuming our walk at a quick pace. I just need to get safely home and away from Adrian.

He keeps up with me as I babble about the best restaurants and bars in every possible direction. I'm flustered and hot and not going to do a thing about it. *Avoid temptation!* I'm only up for casual hookups, and he is not a candidate. Or is he? I stop babbling as I consider this. Maybe it would be casual since he's leaving on Thursday.

But we're friends. Well, we were. A sharp pang of regret makes my chest ache. I lost him and Silvia for so long because of my own protective defenses. My sweet memories of Adrian saw me through so many dark times. Tough Sara who takes care of herself. Never depending on anyone—independent, strong, *alone*.

"You okay?" he asks.

"Yes," I manage. "If you want authentic Cuban food, that's the best place." I point across the street. I'm back on our food tour of Brooklyn that he never asked for.

By the time we get back to my apartment building, I've run out of steam. I cannot say one more word about food, and I'm exhausted from trying to keep myself distracted by his sexy presence as he quietly listens by my side.

I stop in front of my building's door, suddenly awkward over how to say goodbye. Usually this part is a relief for me with a guy and a real quick thing. Maybe I don't want to say goodbye.

He steps close with a smile that lights up his gorgeous face. His voice is warm honey, and I'm melting all over again. "It was really good to see you again, Sara."

I can barely breathe. "You too." I lift my hands at an awkward angle, unsure if we're going for a hug or a handshake.

He takes my hand, lifting it to his lips, and brushes a kiss across my knuckles. I flush with heat, my heart skips a beat, and my stomach flutters. I. Am. Toast. This is so not me. Then again, I've *never* experienced anything sweet like this from a guy. Not since…him.

"See you tomorrow at the game." He holds his hand out, palm up, and wiggles his fingers. "Give me your phone, and I'll add my number."

I fish it out of my purse, unlock it, tap over to contacts, and hand it over. He taps rapidly, his lips curving up in a small smile before he hands it back.

I look at the screen. Instead of Adrian, he added himself as "My Hero." I stare at it for a long moment. I was right. He does have a hero complex. That's why he's been so protective. It's his thing. I shouldn't get carried away with dreamy fantasies that he cares about me.

I meet his eyes. "Seriously?"

He grins. "Remember when I saved you from the sharks?"

I swallow hard, my heart pounding. I can't believe he remembers as much about me as I do about him.

"Sharks? What sharks?"

He tilts his head. "Your poker face could use some work. Admit it, at one point *way-a-y* back I was your hero."

"That was a lifetime ago," I say softly.

"Seems we've got some catching up to do." He salutes me, and for some reason it makes me smile. "Goodnight."

"Goodnight."

I let myself into the building and up to my apartment. The moment I step inside, I ache with loneliness. Ridiculous. I've lived here alone for three weeks now, ever since Chloe moved into her dorm. It's not like I was going to invite him up. Still, I kind of almost miss him. And then, in a rare impulsive move, I pull out my phone and text him.

You were my hero that summer. Sorry. Sometimes old memories bring up good and bad. This is true, though not the main reason I was cagey. I'm just not used to letting anyone in.

No problem. I can be your shark instead. Card shark.

I smile. *So who will save me from you?*

No chance. You're already a goner.

I stare at the words. I know he's joking, but it hits a little too close to home. What if I am a goner? I've never had such an intense physical response to a guy before. I've never melted before either.

I play it cool, my thumbs flying over the keypad. *I'm a card shark too, and it's a shark-eat-shark world.*

Chomp.

I laugh out loud. Chomp.

I text back: *We should play a game just the two of us for old times' sake.* It seems I'm not so good at keeping my distance. Adrian is irresistible.

My cabana has more room. I got a suite in SoHo. Not too long a commute for you.

I smile at the cabana reference. We spent a lot of time playing poker in his cabana. His hotel room is a whole nother level of temptation. I need to be smart. I need to keep my distance.

Maybe.

Chicken.

How many things did I do as a kid because he called me chicken? I shake my head, a reluctant smile tugging at my lips. The boy knew how to get to me. The man is dealing with a different sort of woman. The kind who protects her vulnerable self at all costs.

I text a quick bye. *Goodnight, Adrian.*

Goodnight, Sara, and happy belated twenty-fifth.

I stare at the phone, once again thrown. He's reminding me we're both twenty-five now, and we had a pact. I drop my phone facedown on my futon like it's burning hot.

Chill. It's just the shock of him showing up on your doorstep that has you unsettled. Even so, I put my pajamas on so I won't be tempted to hop on the train and show up at his hotel.

5

Adrian

Sara's game tonight is in a corner lot Victorian mansion in Brooklyn. I didn't know they had mansions in Brooklyn. I thought it was all apartment buildings like in Manhattan. We drove over here together with my guard, and she's early at seven to set up for the eight o'clock game. She says they can run late, sometimes until three in the morning if someone's on a hot streak. Fine by me, I'm a night owl.

She's wearing a pale green blazer, a white blouse, a matching green pencil skirt, and beige heels. She looks fantastic, the clothes accentuating her hourglass shape, but not how I expected her to look for a poker game. She brought a small black wheeled suitcase with her poker stuff inside.

I follow her up the steps of a wide front porch, and we're let in a few moments later by a plump blonde woman in a floral dress. "Welcome, Miss Sara."

"Good to see you again, Ms. Kay," Sara says warmly. "This is Prince Adrian Rourke."

Ms. Kay bows her head and curtsies. "Prince Adrian, welcome."

"Thank you. Nice to meet you, Ms. Kay." I gesture behind me. "This is Jack, my guard. He travels with me everywhere as a precaution. Palace rules."

"Oh! Hello," she says to Jack.

Jack inclines his head. He's not one for conversation or smiles.

Sara steps inside, and we follow her in. There's a curved staircase on our right with a carved wooden handrail, white paneled walls running the length of the staircase. Red and gold carpet cover everything. Very elegant and fitting for a Victorian-era mansion.

"Are we in the parlor again?" Sara asks Ms. Kay.

"Yes, right this way."

We travel down the front hallway past a library on our left to a large parlor the size of two rooms. There's two white carved columns in the center of the space on opposite sides, probably support beams. The parlor has high ceilings, crystal chandeliers, large floor-to-ceiling windows, and crown molding. The furniture is antique. On one side is a seating area with red velvet chairs set in front of a fireplace and, on the other side, a large oval mahogany table with more red velvet chairs. Ten chairs. This must be where they play.

"Let me know if you need anything," Ms. Kay says.

Sara smiles. "I'm expecting food delivery in half an hour. I could use some help setting out the food. Otherwise, we're good."

"Whose house is this?" I ask Sara the moment Ms. Kay steps out. "Where is he?" I'm very curious to meet the guy. It looks like the place of an older man with a family. Definitely not a bachelor pad. Sara told me her players are all young wealthy Russian businessmen.

"It's Ivan's. We rotate spots to keep it interesting. I don't know where he is. Maybe he's upstairs getting ready, or he could be caught at work. He'll be here."

I follow her over to the card table. The top is green leather with brass cup holders and brass chip racks. Really nice. "You'd think he'd be here on time when it's at his place."

"He trusts me to set up. I've been here several times."

"Is he any good?"

"Sure," she says, setting a card shuffler on the table. "They're all good."

I watch as she sets up with her own special card decks and chips. Then she takes a small metal cashbox out and sets it discreetly on an end table in the corner.

"You take that cash home with you?" I ask. "The half mil from the buy-in?"

"It gets paid out, ultimately, to players tomorrow along with the additional bets I collect."

I set my teeth, working to keep my voice even. "And you just walk home by yourself with all that cash in your suitcase?"

"I get a lift home through an app on my phone, easy peasy." She levels me with an irritated look. "I'm not going to walk home in the dark at three a.m. Plus I have pepper spray." At my dubious look, she adds in a low voice, "I can't afford a guard, okay? And that would just draw more attention to me anyway."

I still don't like it, but I keep my mouth shut. I'm here to observe things as they are, not to interfere. I won't press her on anything until *after* I get all the facts.

Jack takes a post in the corner of the room, and I direct him to the other side of the parlor. The last thing I want is for the players to think he's feeding me information. I turn when I hear a masculine voice greeting Sara jovially.

He's thirty at the most with short dark brown hair, wearing a navy blue suit. He smiles as he crosses to her. "What a welcome sight when I return from work," he says with a heavy Russian accent, bending to kiss her cheek. "Sunny Sara."

She smiles brightly. *Sunny Sara.* "Thanks, Ivan! Good to see you too."

"If only I had you here every day when I return home," he says warmly.

I stride toward them to cut off any further flirting.

Sara puts a hand on Ivan's arm. "This is the alternate I told you about, Prince Adrian Rourke."

"Welcome to my humble home, Your Highness," Ivan returns with a bow of his head.

"Thank you." I offer my hand, and he gives me a bone-crunching handshake. Not sure if that's a friendly gesture or not. Handshakes can vary by culture, but something tells me it was a display of power.

"I will change now into something more comfortable," he says and leaves.

"Sunny Sara," I mimic as soon as he's out of earshot.

"It's what I do," she says. "Everything's light and fun with Sunny Sara. I'm the hostess with the mostess."

"What does he do for a living?"

She checks her phone. "He mentioned some kind of importing/exporting with electronics once. They're all successful businessmen."

I lower my voice. "Everything legal in the import/export business?"

"I don't ask questions." She looks up from her phone. "Yuri's going to be an hour late. You're in for the first round."

"Fine by me."

"Have a seat. I'm going to get drinks ready." Before she can do that, another man in his fifties with dark brown hair and light brown skin steps into the parlor. She greets him warmly before turning to me. "This is our dealer, Gustavo," she says. "Gustavo, meet Prince Adrian."

Gustavo bows his head briefly. "Nice to meet you. I've never had royalty at my table."

I smile. "Pretty much like everyone else. Except once in a while I pull out my crown just to make sure all the jewels are still there."

He laughs and heads over to the card table. Sara heads to the kitchen.

I cross to the seating area by the fireplace and pull out my phone, checking on stuff back home. There's several emails from Emma—my formerly silent investor—who's now managing the casino in my place with Jackson. She's aggravated, complaining she doesn't hear about shit until after it's gone south, and then there's nothing she can do about it. *Welcome to my world!* I'm glad it's not just me. She also says the restaurant didn't keep enough inventory of lobster, which is really dumb because that's one of Villroy's major exports.

The flowers she ordered never arrived, but she was charged for them anyway. And a male guest patted her ass when she stopped by a blackjack table to inquire if everyone was enjoying themselves. Jackson took that guy out before security could even get close.

Well, well, well. Not easy to take a walk in my shoes. I know it's wrong, but I'm glad she's not having an easy go of it. I was beginning to think it was me that was the problem, instead of it just being a really demanding job.

Sara and Ms. Kay return to the parlor with trays filled with shot glasses, vodka, and pickles. Interesting.

A short while later, the food arrives. I thought it would be some traditional Russian food, but instead she ordered dim sum, a cheese platter with olives and crackers, and individual dishes of meatballs. Ms. Kay arrives with caviar from the kitchen and some dark crackers.

"Do you vary the menu each game?" I ask Sara.

"Yes. It's always a surprise, and I try to get light little appetizers. I don't want anyone sluggish at the game. Just small bites to keep them alert and having a good time. These are from a foodie service. They stop at the best restaurants in the neighborhood and deliver."

"What other kinds of foods do you get from a foodie service?"

"We have a lot of ethnicities here. Could be Caribbean, Russian, Jewish, Italian. We've got pretty much everything. I avoid pizza due to the heaviness factor."

"And you stick to vodka. No beer or wine."

She lifts a shoulder. "I tried beer, but they just prefer vodka. They like to toast a lot. Keep your glass in the air until the toast is completely done and drink it all at once. That's the custom."

"I'm aware. Is everyone hammered at the end of the night?"

"No. It's a small shot, they eat between shots, and they've got a tolerance, I guess."

"And you?"

She leans close and whispers, "Sometimes I spit it back

into my chaser drink of cranberry juice. Usually it's just me or the occasional woman one of them brings along that have the chaser. The guys prefer their vodka straight up."

"You really took the time to understand their culture, didn't you?"

"There's a huge Russian community in Brighton Beach, one of the Brooklyn neighborhoods. I was already familiar with their culture and, believe me, they let me know loud and clear when they like something or don't."

The rest of the guys arrive within minutes of each other, and Sara introduces me to them. They look a little starstruck, bowing and staring at me, so I try to put them at ease, thanking them for letting me join their game in Yuri's absence. There's Mikhail, Alexy, Roman, Kirill, Vlad, Sergei, and two Dmitris.

Then I'm temporarily lost, as the conversation is entirely in Russian. I wonder if Sara knows what they're saying and how much she misses during the game that could indicate a problem she doesn't know about. Ignorance is not bliss when it comes to high-stakes poker games.

I watch as they each greet Sara warmly, kissing her cheek and calling her Sunny Sara. She's bright, warm, and friendly. They all want her. I'm not being paranoid. Guys know this kind of thing. She's single and sexy, and there are no girl-friends here. It's nine guys in their twenties and thirties, some in casual T-shirts and jeans, some in dress shirts and trousers, all surreptitiously checking her out, from her perky breasts to her narrow waist and the flare of hips clearly outlined by her outfit. Only I can check her out because I'm her hero. I look out for her while battling my own lust. That's damn heroic all by itself.

Sara casually shifts to the corner with the cashbox. They're in good spirits as they follow her, each handing over a wad of cash for their buy-in, which she accepts while chatting with them as if the money is beside the point.

I hand her my cash last. She doesn't make conversation with me, just quietly tucks the cash inside, locks the box, and stashes it in her suitcase. The men are talking to each other like they're old friends, occasionally slapping each other on the back. I'm curious how they make their money, but I play it cool. I'll see how things play out.

First, everyone raids the food table, talking loudly. Sara doesn't join them, instead sitting casually near the card table with a pleasant expression on her face like she enjoys watching them enjoying themselves. I help myself to some dim sum. No one talks to me, though I get some friendly smiles and head nods. I hesitate to interrupt their conversation in Russian. After everyone eats, Sara pours vodka into the shot glasses. This seems to be an indicator that the game will begin, because plates are left on the side table and everyone wanders over to the card table with their drinks.

Ivan stands next to the game table. "Before we play, a toast." He lifts his glass high in the air, and we all follow suit.

Ivan lifts his glass toward Sara and then me. "To our hostess with the mostess and her royal friend."

Everyone clinks glasses and downs the shot. *Ho-yah! Bu-u-urn.* I suppress a grimace. I'm more of a beer drinker than vodka, but when in Brooklyn...

Finally, everyone takes a seat at the card table. Sara announces the round to a jovial cheer from the guys.

The dealer begins, and the conversation is in English now, probably because of me. The guys banter back and forth over who's been eating too much pizza and putting on a paunch.

I'm prepared to lose, but I have to make it look good, not like I did it on purpose.

Half the guys are easy to read, looking at their hole cards immediately after they're dealt, their expressions pleased or disappointed. I'm not the only one catching their tells. Two of the players play like pros—emotionless but observant.

"Have you been playing together long?" I ask casually.

"Since August," Alexy says. "Ivan got the introduction to Sara through Sergei. We all knew each other in different ways, gradually bringing it to ten."

"We started with five," Sara says. "I think ten's more fun, don't you?"

"I like it," Alexy says.

There's a round of agreement and then someone proposes another toast to the ten of them. I take the shot and catch Sara slip off to the corner for her juice chaser. I bet she spit that one out. I'm feeling really warm and relaxed now. I should get myself a chaser too, so I don't veer into drunk territory and lose sight of my purpose here. I don't care if the guys never do chasers. As my twin likes to point out when I do what I want, I'm comfortable enough in my masculinity to pull it off. Besides, I'm on a mission to make sure Sara isn't in danger. He-man enough right there. Ha!

I don't want to get up from the table, so I signal to Sara with a really obvious drink gesture, tipping my imaginary glass to my lips.

"More vodka!" Ivan calls to Sara. "The prince needs more vodka."

"Juice chaser would be good too," I say, sending her a meaningful look.

She grins. "I'm on it."

I stick to Sara's method of using the juice chaser to casually spit my vodka into for the next shot. No one gives me shit about the chaser. They're all having a great time.

An hour later, I've lost on purpose, and a few of the guys have triumphant gleams in their eyes. I don't lose a horrible amount. Just enough to make everyone happy.

Sara stays quietly standing in the background, looking like she's enjoying being here as host. She doesn't comment on wins or losses, only chiming in when they address her, which becomes more frequent as the night goes on. All warm friendly talk. No one's out of line, so I relax.

Yuri arrives, a tall man in his twenties with slicked-back dark brown hair and a neatly trimmed beard. The guys greet him cheerfully. Sara introduces us, and then I step away from the table so he can take my place. I head over to Sara. Normally, I'd leave once I'm done playing, but I want to stick close to Sara to see how things play out.

"Everyone's having a good time," I say to her in a low voice.

"That's the plan," she says cheerfully. "A good time for all. I saw what you did there with the juice chaser."

"Yeah, well, it was a good idea you had." I return my attention to the game. I need to find out last names so I can look into everyone later, just to be sure everything is okay.

The night passes uneventfully. Just guys having a good time. It's late when Yuri makes his move, asking the guys if they want to get in on a real estate deal. He only has a slight accent. "Prince Adrian, you could join in too. I've got a lead on some industrial land in Queens. It's a sure thing. Queens is like the next Brooklyn. You'd get your investment back five-fold." He passes his business cards around the table and leaves one for me on the end, tapping it with his fingers and inclining his head toward me.

"I'm investing in my homeland right now, but I'll think about it," I say, striding over and tucking the card in my pocket just for reference. Now I have a last name for Yuri to look up later.

He nods and turns back to the guys, switching to Russian. There seems to be some interest and a few nods. Real estate in nearby Queens sounds legit to me. Maybe Silvia was worried for nothing.

The game ends with Sergei in a snit over his loss, throwing his cards down and challenging Ivan to a fistfight. He says it in English, and I suspect it's because he wants Sara to know what he's up to.

Sara steps in right on cue, smoothing things over. "It's late. Game will be back on Thursday. More fun, more chances to win. How about we raise the buy-in to one hundred K? Makes it that much easier to recoup quickly."

Sergei huffs, his dark eyes murderous on Ivan. "Be a man and step outside."

Ivan grabs him by the shirt collar and hauls him up close. "Get out of my home. You are no longer welcome here."

Sara hovers nearby. "Next game is in a hotel suite. Perfect for everyone. Sergei, I *really* hope to see you there." There's a hint of flirtation in her voice.

Sergei yanks Ivan's hands off him and straightens his

dress shirt. He turns to Sara. "I will be there for you, beautiful Sara."

"See you then," Sara says with a sunny smile. "Goodnight."

He swaggers out the door.

Does she always handle the guys by being flirty?

The moment we're safely back in the car on the way to her apartment, I ask, "How many times have you been asked out by one of the guys?"

She waves a hand airily. "Don't worry about it. Harmless flirting. Everyone knows I don't date a player, or do anything else with them. It's strictly poker and friendship."

"And how do they know that?"

She sighs. "Because, if they ask me out, that's what I tell them."

"Who asked you out?"

"Just Sergei, and yes, I explained my policy of keeping it professional."

I clench my jaw, a rare stab of jealousy making me more irritated than I have a right to be. Sara isn't mine. I force my mind back to my purpose tonight. I don't think her players are organized crime—they seem like regular guys—but I also don't think she's out of danger. I'm concerned about the risk she takes handling the money, both by taking the buy-in home with her and by covering their bets.

I open my mouth to address the money issue, but what comes out is a growl of possessiveness that surprises even me. "Don't talk to them in a flirty way. They'll get the wrong idea."

She exhales sharply. "Jesus, Adrian. What is this? I can talk however I want to. Sweet goes a lot further with these guys. I'm the one who keeps it light and fun."

"By using their attraction to you?"

She lifts one shoulder. "I can't help it if guys are attracted to me. That's their problem. Not mine."

"So you don't find any of them attractive?"

She rolls her eyes. "They're all attractive. It doesn't matter. I'm there for the game and the tips. I don't date players."

I calm down a little. I reassure myself that what I thought was jealousy was actually more protectiveness than anything else. "How much did you collect in tips tonight?" I saw the guys handing her chips and wads of bills as they each took their leave.

Her face lights up. "Sixty K. Some of them were extra happy to have you at the game and also glad to be in on a sure thing with the land development deal. They were feeling extra generous."

Her suitcase of money is safely in the trunk of the car, but anyone who knew about her game could track her down at her apartment and take it. She lives alone. She's small, shorter than my sister. My protective instincts are perfectly justified in this case.

"You need a guard," I say. "I don't like you handling the money by yourself."

"I told you I can't afford that. I'll look into it as soon as I have enough for Chloe's tuition. I need to save enough to get her through undergrad; then I can consider spending else-where. It's a calculated risk."

I keep my voice even. "I'll cover the cost of a guard."

"No, I'm not taking your money. It's fine. I only have the money in hand for a short time and then it goes in my safe."

"Your safe," I echo. "And how hard would it be to get you to open that safe if someone broke in?" My mind goes to a dark place, and I don't like the risk she's taking at all.

She clamps her mouth shut and looks straight ahead.

I press on. "And what if one of the players became aggres-sive after the game? Sergei almost had a fight."

She shakes her head. "I know how to talk to these guys. Besides, I'm the key to their game. They love it. And every one of them is thrilled to be there. I actually had to turn some guys away. I screened them for deep pockets and playing ability ahead of time. It's an honor to be at a Sara Travers game."

I still don't like it, but I'll wait and see how it plays out tomorrow when she's collecting and doling out money. She may not be mine now, but she's still my Sara from golden carefree summers. Nothing can happen to her.

I give her hair a tug. It's as silky soft as it looks. "An honor to be at a Sara Travers game. Wow, aren't you something special?"

She grins. "I am. So do you feel better about my game now? Report back to Silvia that all is well."

"I want to watch collections tomorrow. Then I'll report back."

She stiffens. "You can't come into people's places with me on collections. They hate to be the loser who has to pay up. I have to keep it like a fun social visit. The last thing they'll want is another guy witnessing it."

"I'll wait in the car. If anyone gives you trouble, I'll be nearby with Jack."

Her green eyes flash. "There's not going to be any trouble, except for the trouble *you* might cause by being there."

"I'll be discreet."

She crosses her arms. "Sorry, but a black Mercedes with tinted windows isn't exactly discreet."

"They all live in wealthy neighborhoods, right?"

"Yeah."

"So it should fit right in."

She narrows her eyes. "Your car sticks out. Most of them don't own cars. They walk or use a ride app. A car's a hassle in Brooklyn."

"Tell them I'm your boyfriend, and we're going out afterward."

"I'm not going to tell them that."

The car pulls up to her place. I get out and get her suitcase for her, intending to see her safely inside with it. "I'm walking you in," I inform her.

She sighs. "Fine."

I follow her upstairs and watch her dig her key out of her purse by her apartment door. "So why won't you tell them I'm your boyfriend? Don't you know I'm a catch?"

She shakes her head. "Ya know, for someone who's been

here for, like, two seconds, you're awfully pushy about the way I do business." She opens her door.

I follow her in and set her suitcase next to the coffee table. "So?"

She locks the door and turns back to me. A tense beat passes, our eyes locked.

Her voice is breathy. "So it's a lie. You're not my boyfriend." She looks up at me under her lashes, a pink flush to her cheeks. She wants me to kiss her.

I lower my voice to a husky tone. I may be aggravated with the risk she's taking, but I'm also deeply drawn to her. She's like the missing piece to a puzzle, the perfect fit I hadn't known I was searching for until I found her again. "So kiss me and make it the truth." It's a dare and an invitation. *I want you.*

She steps closer. "I'm not kissing you."

"Bet you're too damn scared." *Kiss me.*

"I don't operate on a bet anymore."

I close the distance. Sara Travers can't resist me. "Shame. You were more fun when you did." *Let's see what you got.*

Her eyes widen, and then she grabs my head and kisses me hard on the lips. A surge of triumph shoots through me.

She pulls back, and we eye each other. We both want more. I can feel it.

She kisses me again, softer now, her hand resting on my cheek. "Adrian."

I slide my hand into her silky hair and take the kiss I've been aching for. It's hot and hungry. I'm greedy for more, my arms wrapping around her, bringing her close.

Next thing I know we're on her futon, and she's straddling my lap, her skirt hiked up to her hips, her fingers gripping my hair, kissing me urgently. It's heaven and hell at the same time. I need so much more.

She breaks the kiss, breathing hard, her fingers tangled in my hair. "I swore I wouldn't do this."

I stroke my fingers down her throat. Her pulse is beating rapidly. So's mine. "Why not?"

"Because..." She swallows visibly, looking away. One of

her tells—avoiding eye contact. "Because I want to remember you as part of my sweet past."

I kiss her gently. "Tell me the truth. Why not?" If she's really opposed to exploring what may be between us, I'll back off.

"That's the truth," she insists, staring at my mouth.

I have a feeling there's more to it, like maybe she still has me tangled up with Villroy and those associations with her parents, but I'll have to wait until she's ready to say it.

I hold her jaw, stroking her soft cheek with my thumb. "I'll always be part of your past. That's how time works. Past is the past. Present is…" I nuzzle into her neck, working my way up to her ear, breathing in her sweet scent before I give the lobe a tug with my teeth. "Right here, right now. I want you."

Her green eyes are dilated. She wants me too. I love that I can read her so easily. "For how long?"

"Until we're both gasping for air."

6

She smiles and gets off my lap, yanking her skirt back in place. "I think it's better if we don't get tangled up that way."

Damn, I lost her. I barely resist grabbing her and hauling her back. "I like getting tangled up that way."

She smooths her hair. "Well, so do I, but then it'll be awkward and you'll leave, and it just sounds messy. Let's keep things neat between us."

A beat passes in silence as we eye each other once more, the tension thick in the air.

I stand in front of her, close but not too close. "Aren't you curious how we'd be together? I mean, I know a lot more about women now than when I was twelve. You liked my first kiss enough to propose to me." I grin.

She puts her hand over my mouth. "Not another word, you tempting devil. And I proposed *before* the kiss."

"Because I was your hero." I take her hand and kiss her palm and then the sensitive underside of her wrist. She shivers. I release her hand, and she stares straight ahead.

"You play dirty," she says in a hoarse voice.

"Play with me."

"Adrian!"

"Sara!"

She takes off her blazer and sets it neatly across her arm. "No."

"Okay."

Her brows shoot up over wide eyes. "Really?"

"Yeah, really. I'll just play by myself. Want to watch?"

She laughs.

This is going to be torture. I want her even more now that I've had a taste. I can be patient. Really. I can.

"Put your money in your safe and then I'll go," I tell her.

"But then you'll know where I stash my money."

"You really think I'm going to steal from you?"

Her cheeks tinge with pink. "Sorry. No. I'm just naturally distrustful of people."

"I'm not people. I'm your hero."

She wags her finger at me as she heads to the tiny kitchen. "You keep saying that."

"Because it's true."

I watch her pull the safe from the oven. Not a bad hiding place considering the limited places where she could hide something in her apartment.

She gathers the money and chips from her suitcase, sets them on the coffee table, and then sits on the futon with the safe, about to do the combination. "Don't look."

I sit next to her on the futon and slap a hand over my eyes. "Your secret code is safe with me. Let me guess, Chloe's birthday."

"How did you know?"

I drop my hand. "You just told me, and it's not hard to guess. Use something random."

"But then how will I remember it?"

"You'll remember it because it's important."

She opens the safe and quickly shoves tonight's tips in there. I spy stacks of hundreds with rubber bands and some cards sticking up in the back. Wait a minute. Is that what I think it is?

I stare at her in shock. "You still have them. The pair of red twos." It must mean something. She keeps them in her safe like they're valuable. Did she hope we'd reunite one day?

She flushes bright red, peeks in the safe, and hastily slides the cards under the bills. "I need to get a bigger safe."

I lean close. "You pretended you didn't remember the pact, but you kept the pair."

She bites her lower lip. "They're my lucky cards."

"Why?" For the first time, I'm hopeful. Like maybe it's a sign we were meant to be. I thought she'd shut me out of her life for good, until I came barging back in, but maybe she never let me go, just like I never managed to let her go.

She quickly shuts the safe and locks it. "They remind me of a simpler time when I believed in heroes."

I cup the back of her neck, pulling her close and pressing a kiss to her lips. "I'm here now."

She pulls away and stands with her safe clutched to her chest. "It's different now. I'm different. You should go." She heads for the kitchen and puts her safe back in the oven.

I'm not sure what to say or do, still reeling from the discovery that Sara held onto those cards. She held onto our connection.

"Please go," she says quietly.

I stand. "I'm going, but I'll be back."

She lifts her hand in a brief wave and turns away, but not before I see the shine of tears in her eyes. I halt. Why the tears? She must have some feeling for me. Why is she upset about it? Does she think I'm going to leave for good? Because if there's something there between us, something real, I'm open to seeing where it goes. I'm torn between hauling her into my arms and giving her the space she asked for.

I step toward the door, giving her one last look. Her arms are crossed now, hugging herself. I can't leave her like this.

I cross to her, tip her chin up and kiss her gently. "I'm glad we met again and, if you'll let me, I want to stay in your life."

Her green eyes are shiny, her lips pressed tightly together. "Ade, I've changed. I can't do relationships. I'm broken."

I stroke her hair back. "I always say relationships are a bad bet, but we go back so far it's not even fair to call it a relationship. It's more like we just picked up where we left off."

She stares at me, her brow crinkled in apparent thought.

I want to say more, that I could never commit to anyone, and maybe that was because no one could compare to her. Maybe I'm making too much of the pair of twos she held onto, but this feels right.

I cup her jaw, and her eyes go soft. She definitely has some feeling for me. "I kept my pair of fives too."

She swallows visibly, her cheeks flushing pink. "You did?"

"Of course. We had a pact." I give her a quick hard kiss and leave before I can get caught up in her again.

~

Sara

Last night with Adrian got intense. I can't believe he hung onto his pair of fives! Is it possible he held onto our shared fantasy future just like I did? Did it bring a bright spot to dark times for him too? No. Adrian didn't have dark times. He lives a golden life, a royal with a large loving family, who does whatever he wants. He says he wants to be in my life, but I know he's tied to Villroy, and I never want to go there again. It's just too painful with all the memories of my parents. I can't face that grief again. I just can't. It was hard enough the first time. Besides, I have a good thing going here with my game, and I could never leave Chloe.

I can't let him get close enough to make the goodbye painful. He's decided to stay an extra day, and I'm trying not to read too much into it. I need to keep a friendly affection between us and then go back to my life.

Adrian showed up this morning just like he said he would. Part of me was glad because I missed him after he left last night, and part of me was irritated that he's checking up on the way I do business. Today is collection and payout day for the game, and we're in his rented Mercedes on the way to my first collection. His guard, Jack, is in the front passenger seat. Adrian doesn't know what it's like to truly be on your own and know there's no one you can depend on besides yourself.

I direct the driver, Bill, to park a short way down the block from the brownstone I'm going to and then hop out of the car, feeling Adrian's eyes on me. He'll probably time how long I'm inside the place too. He and his guard will storm the brownstone if I'm not out in the requisite amount of time. I stifle a sigh. I'm not used to having someone second-guess me. Honestly, these guys are not dangerous. Okay, I had a dicey moment with Sergei on collection day before, only because he was angling for a date, but he backed off. Of course, it's a good idea to have someone guarding the money as I travel with it, but I just can't justify paying a guard when I know Chloe's tuition bill is so hefty.

The first visit goes smoothly, and I can't help but rub it in Adrian's face when I get back in the car. "I told you. No big thing. I keep it a light, fun visit."

His expression gives nothing away, poker face firmly in place. "Sure. Let me know when we're at Sergei's place."

"He's a sore loser. Doesn't mean he won't pay up. He's loaded."

"Tell him we're together now." He says it matter-of-factly like he expects me to comply. It gets my back up. Bad enough he's got his nose in my business; now he's issuing orders.

"I'm not going to say that. You're leaving in two days, anyway, so it's not like that's a deterrent." I huff. "You know this kind of bossiness may work with your sister, but it's not gonna fly with me. I've been operating just fine on my own for a very long time."

He tucks a lock of hair behind my ear in a tender gesture, his voice deep and warm. "I wish I'd known you then. I feel like I missed so much."

I swallow over the lump in my throat. Somehow he cuts through all my defenses so easily. "You wouldn't have wanted to know me then. It was hell, and I was not fun to be around."

"I could've helped you."

"No one could've helped me and, believe me, they tried. My uncle, my school social worker, my teachers. I had to pull myself together, and I did it by focusing on caring for Chloe, which was a win-win for both of us." I paste on a smile and gesture to myself. "Count yourself lucky to meet the newly put together Sara."

His eyes are so sympathetic, I have to look away. I hate sympathy. I've had way too much of it in my life, along with the whispers: "Those poor Travers girls. Such a shame, and their uncle isn't much help."

I force my mind back to business. The next stop goes smoothly. This time I stifle the *I told you so*, but I sure am thinking it.

A few minutes later, I tell the driver, "Turn right at the stop sign. It's at the end of the next block."

"Is this Sergei's place?" Adrian asks.

I'm a little surprised he guessed. "How did you know?"

"Because only three people owed you after the buy-in was collected, and we already made two stops. Process of elimination."

"Such a smartie. Stay here."

He arches a brow but says nothing.

When I get to Sergei's house, I ring the bell and wait on the front stoop. I hear stealthy footsteps behind me and whirl, about to yell at Adrian to back off, but it's Jack.

"I'm to accompany you inside, ma'am," he says.

"You can't. I won't be able to collect with another guy witnessing it."

His expression is unyielding. "I'll remain in the background completely unobtrusively. I won't even look at him."

I stifle a groan. "Go away. Please. This is going to make things so much worse."

The front door opens and it's Sergei, not the housekeeper. "Good morning, Sara. Looks like you brought some muscle today. Don't trust me to honor my debt?"

"Of course I trust you. My—" I nearly choke on the word "—boyfriend is insanely overprotective and insisted his guard accompany me today." I don't have boyfriends. I have acquaintances.

"Prince Adrian is your boyfriend?"

I nod. It's all I can manage.

His eyes narrow. "You said you would never consider

being with a player. Now you are telling me that Prince Adrian, a player, is someone you are with."

"He's a temporary guest, not a permanent player. We've known each other for a very long time."

He looks up and down the street and spots the Mercedes sitting conspicuously a few doors down. "Is that him?"

Before I can deny it, Sergei strides outside and goes right to the car, knocking on the driver's side window.

Adrian steps out of the backseat. "How's it going?"

Sergei crosses his arms, his legs braced wide apart in battle stance. "It's going shitty. I've lost two games in a row, and now there are three people here to witness it. I want you all gone."

Adrian's gaze turns steely. "Pay up and we'll go."

Sergei turns and storms back to his place. I rush after him, but he slams the door in my face. I hear the snick of the lock. Fuck.

I ring the bell again and again. He owes me too much to walk away. One hundred K. It'll clean me out to cover him. I glare at Adrian, who's standing on the sidewalk nearby. "You screwed it up!" I shout at him. "I've never had a problem before now."

"This was always a possibility," he says calmly.

I turn back to the door and pound on it. His housekeeper, Ms. Davies, answers. "I'm sorry, Miss Sara. Sergei isn't taking callers right now."

"Please. I just need to talk to him." I open my purse and dig out a hundred-dollar bill from my last collection visit and press it in her hand. "Here, for your trouble."

She gives me a look of disgust and hands it back. "I'll lose my job for not following orders."

I shove past her and rush down the hallway. He's probably in his study. "Sergei!"

Footsteps pound behind me. Oh, shit. It's like I have a parade. Jack, Adrian, and Ms. Davies are following me at a run. "Stay back!" I shout. "This is business!"

I find the study and there he is, sitting at his desk. I quickly shut the door behind me and lock it. "Sorry about the disturbance earlier. It's just you and me now. Let's get straight and then we'll be good for Thursday."

Someone knocks on the door. "Go away!" I shout.

"I told her not to come in," Ms. Davies says through the door. "Very sorry, Sergei. She overpowered me and forced her way in."

Sergei sends me a dark look. "That is my aunt's friend."

"I didn't overpower her," I whisper fiercely. "I just ran past her."

"Please leave us," Sergei commands loud enough to be heard by the crowd on the other side of the door.

Ms. Davies speaks softly through the door. "As you wish, sir."

He stares at his desk morosely.

"It's okay," I say, approaching cautiously. "I'm sure you'll do great next game. Odds are in your favor, right? Nowhere to go but up."

He exhales sharply. "I don't have the money."

My stomach drops. "What do you mean you don't have the money?"

He lifts his head. "I gave Yuri the last of my reserves for his sure-thing land deal. Everything else is gone. You must understand. His investment was worth more to me than paying a poker game debt."

I hold onto my temper. "Sergei, if you don't pay, then the winners don't get their full winnings. They'll quit. The game will fold."

He lifts one shoulder in a careless shrug. "I don't want Ivan to have my money anyway. He's swinging his dick around, showing off with his mansion and his diamond cuff links."

I lose it. "He was wearing a T-shirt and jeans! And you have a mansion too!"

He scowls. "I've seen him wear the diamond cuff links. And my town house is not a mansion. I need my money more than he does."

I take a deep breath. "I can't cover you. This is it. If you don't pay, you can't play in the game anymore."

He lifts a shoulder. "Your boyfriend could take my place in the game."

I reach for calm. "That doesn't erase your debt. Listen, how about half? Can you cover half?"

He lifts his palms. "I'm afraid not. Please shut the door on your way out."

"You're out," I say in a low, controlled voice. "I have a waiting list. I wish it didn't have to be this way."

"Business," he says. "Sometimes it's good; sometimes it's bad."

I swear he's stiffing me as payback for turning him down. I turn on my heel and stride toward the door. My hand's on the knob when he says, "Call me when your boyfriend leaves your bed cold again. Now that I'm not a player, you can be with me."

I knew it! He's mad I turned him down, and seeing Adrian here made it worse.

I shake my head and turn. "I will never be with you."

"I still care for you, Sunny Sara."

Blech.

I open the door and find Adrian and Jack standing just on the other side of it. Adrian's eyes are knowing. He said this would happen, that I'd get stiffed one day and come up short. I always knew it was a risk to front their bets myself, but I always came out even the next day. Only this time I had an entourage with me and everything went south. I could've convinced Sergei if I didn't have curious witnesses. It put him on edge.

I brush past Adrian and Jack and stride out the door. This sucks. Every time I get ahead, something pulls me right back to square one.

Adrian catches up to me on the sidewalk. "I'll help cover him."

"No! You've done enough." I look down the street. "I'm walking home."

"Come on. You knew this was a possibility. At some point a player was going to stiff you. So it happened."

"It happened because you were there! And your guard. I could've gotten it out of him."

He shakes his head. "You think flirting is going to get your players to cough up the money? That only goes so far. Especially after turning him down."

I make a frustrated half scream, turn, and stride down the street.

Adrian keeps up with me. "Sara, you're carrying more than half a mil in your purse, and you think you can just walk all the way back to your apartment by yourself with that?"

"Shh. Nobody knows what I have until you blab about it."

"Silvia was worried about you, and now I am too."

I halt. "Don't you see? I have *nothing* to lose and everything to gain. My life before this sucked, okay? I worked two jobs, exhausted all the time, for crap pay. Maybe that's something a prince doesn't know about, living it up at the palace, but for people stuck here in the real world, that's how it is. You work and work and work and you barely have enough to pay your bills. I was an office manager and a waitress. Two jobs! And I could barely survive. I brought Chloe food from my one comped meal a day at the diner because we could barely afford groceries. Can you picture that?"

His eyes are sympathetic. "It sounds tough."

"Ya think? Or…you get creative, take a risk, and finally get somewhere. That's where I was, and now you're trying to drag me back down to the muck again."

"Are you done?"

I blow out a breath. "Yeah, that about covers it."

His voice is a gruff command. "Get in the car."

I hesitate.

"If you don't, my car will follow you all the way home, so you may as well take the easy way."

I close my eyes for a moment. "Fine. You suck."

"Thanks."

I get in the car, and he follows me in, takes my hand in his, and gives it a warm squeeze. My eyes get hot. I still remember when he held my hand all the way to the health clinic when I was in pain and terrified of stitches in my ankle.

He cares about me, and it's been so long since I've felt cared for. It makes my insides quiver, unsure if I can trust this feeling enough to enjoy it.

"Listen, I want you to land on your feet," he says. "I don't want you in the muck either. Come back to Villroy with me. I could use you at the casino. I need a pit boss. Someone who understands gambling, who can make the staff feel comfortable. I'll give you a generous salary; you can stay at the palace in a guest room. We'll commute together. It will all be so much easier *and safer* than what you're doing here."

I go cold. Villroy is the last place I want to be. "I stand on my own two feet, and I don't need a handout."

"You'd be doing me a favor. I need a right-hand woman. I'm so sick of all the phone calls, texts, and emails, and the day-to-day stuff with staff is not my thing. I want to be working on big-picture strategies for running the place and bringing in more business. You could be good at it. Your experience is perfect. An office manager slash card shark slash waitress? It's like my dream candidate."

I laugh a little. No one has ever called me a dream in any context. "I can't. Chloe needs me." It's true. She's my responsibility. And Villroy is never going to happen. I want to be past this—it's been twelve years since I lost my parents—but I'm just not. Even now my chest aches just thinking about them. I can't lose control to panic attacks again.

Adrian presses on. "Chloe's at university. She's an adult."

I shake my head. "It's different with us. She barely remembers our parents. She was only six when they died. I'm like a mom to her. I visit her once a week, and we text all the time. She needs to know I'm only a train ride away. I'm all she has."

He gazes into my eyes for a long moment. "Just promise me you'll think about it."

I sigh. "Okay, I'll think about it." But I already know I can't leave Chloe, and I can't face the memories of my parents on Villroy. It was the best, most happiest times our family had, and it'll hurt too much to feel their absence there. My chest tightens, and I let out a breath I didn't realize I was holding. I do that. Just stop breathing when the memory of them gets too intense. *Breathe in, breathe out. I'm in control.*

And then Adrian surprises me, wrapping an arm around me and pulling me close. My head rests against his chest. I'm frozen in shock for a moment. He smooths my hair back with his other hand and gives me a smile, his hazel eyes warm on mine.

Oh God, I'm going to cry. I close my eyes tight, willing my tears away. I can't get used to this. It'll be too painful to say goodbye.

I start to get up, and his arm tightens around me. "Just a little longer," he murmurs. "I've missed you. Every woman I've met since you has paled in comparison."

My heart thunders in my chest. I can't believe he just said that. It's so sweet, so…romantic. I can't even find it in me to be angry anymore that he fucked up the Sergei situation.

The words are on the tip of my tongue. *I missed you too.* But I can't speak past the lump in my throat. For so long I hadn't wanted to connect with any reminders of family summers on Villroy, but meeting Adrian here on my territory makes it a lot easier.

I cuddle closer and breathe him in, spice and man. A good man. Maybe he's the reason I've never stayed with any man. I was just waiting to meet him again.

7

Adrian

After Sara made good on her winners' share of the money —drawing from her own stash of cash despite my offer to help—I went to visit my twin for lunch in Manhattan. Silvia was her usual affectionate, enthusiastic self and invited me for dinner at her place tonight, along with Sara and Chloe. She called it "an impromptu dinner party." I told her to make the arrangements and I'd be there. Sara will find it harder to say no to Silvia's invitation than mine. I know I've been pushy, sticking my nose into Sara's life, but it's the only way for me to figure out what's going on with her game and the players in it. I'm staying an extra day so I can go to Sara's Thursday night game.

Okay, she's the reason I'm staying. I want more time to convince her to consider the job at my casino.

Next order of business—and it's a big one—Silvia gave me my cousin Dylan's info. He lives in Brooklyn, working construction for his uncle's company. A far cry from his rightful inheritance. If his father hadn't abdicated the throne, Dylan would've been the crown prince, heir to the kingdom of Villroy. He's the firstborn. By all rights, Dylan should be king. He's a year older than Gabriel, our current king.

I text him on the ride back to my hotel. *Hi, this is Adrian,*

Silvia Rourke's twin. She gave me your number. I'm in town and was hoping to meet up. I wanted to ask you about some locals in a friend's poker game.

A text comes back hours later. It's simply an address in Brooklyn. Five o'clock.

Okay. Not exactly friendly, but maybe he's busy at work. Silvia's dinner party is at seven. Maybe I could invite him too. She wouldn't mind.

I text a quick reply. *See you then.*

I show up at the appointed time, and it's a construction site by the waterfront. A huge crew is filtering out from the site because it's quitting time. I don't know which one he is. I'm looking for someone who resembles my family. Tall, dark haired, maybe with the famous Rourke aquamarine eyes. My father always said they were a sign of the true rulers of Villroy because they match the sea there. Silvia, Emma, and I inherited my mother's hazel eyes. Good thing we were born later down the line or that would've shot that superstition to hell.

I text Dylan. *Where are you? I'm here.*

Meet me at Tazza Café.

I look around and spot the café across the street. I head over with my guard, Jack, trailing me, and go inside. I don't see anyone who looks like they're in construction in here. Just a few hipster types with laptops. Now I'm getting irritated.

I find a table in the back and text him to let him know where I'm sitting. Jack stands in the corner adjacent to me.

Finally, a guy walks in who I think could be him. He's in his thirties, tall and fit in a blue Byrne Construction T-shirt, jeans, and black work boots. His black hair is on the longish side, his cheekbones sharp, his square jaw sporting a neatly trimmed beard. A tribal tattoo over one bulging bicep peeks out of his shirtsleeve. Royals can't have tattoos in my kingdom. It's considered desecration of the body, and we wouldn't be buried in the royal plot because of it. Dylan has unknowingly made it so he's denied his place in death there, after being denied his place there in life. It strikes me as horribly unfair. I hadn't given much thought to it before. It was simply a fact—my uncle's family was exiled. They were foggy in my mind, there were no pictures of them at home, but seeing him here in the flesh, it strikes me how wrong it is.

I stand, adrenaline rushing through me. I'm about to meet my long-lost cousin! "Dylan?"

He strides over and stops in front of me. His eyes are a piercing blue, not the Rourke aquamarine. He stares for a moment, taking me in. "You're not cute like your twin."

I bark out a laugh. "I don't aspire to be cute." I gesture toward my table. "Have a seat."

"I'm gonna get a sandwich first. Want anything?"

He's strangely casual about meeting me for the first time. Maybe it's to cover the awkwardness of the situation, or maybe that's just how laid-back he always is.

"Actually, Silvia is having me and a couple of friends over for dinner tonight. You're welcome to join us."

He doesn't accept or decline. "I skipped lunch. Gotta eat."

"I'll take an espresso, thanks." I pull my wallet out, but he holds up a palm, declining the gesture.

I take a seat. Another surreal moment—my long-lost cousin is buying me an espresso. My first surreal moment was seeing Sara Travers after so many years. I'm excited to meet him and hope to meet his brothers and parents too.

He takes a seat a few minutes later, shoving my espresso across the table to me. "That your muscle?" he asks, jerking his chin toward Jack.

"I have a guard, yes. Sometimes people are overzealous. I haven't had any issues since I arrived in New York."

He takes a bite of roast beef sandwich. After he chews, he says, "Yeah, give it time. You show your face enough, the paps will show up."

I take a sip of espresso, thinking we should get back to the basics. I mean, this is a big moment—long-lost cousins meeting for the first time. "It's great to meet you. Silvia told me about you and your brothers. It's strange to have cousins I've never met."

He lifts his gaze to mine. "Not so strange. Your family

kicked us out for good. Kinda squashed the idea of any reunions."

I lean forward. "Things are different now at the palace. My oldest brother, Gabriel, is king now. His wife is an American, a very down-to-earth woman. Maybe now that they're in charge, they'd be open to you and your family coming for a visit."

He snorts. "Yeah."

"Really. I'll make it right. You should see where you came from."

He takes a big bite of sandwich and chews.

I press on. "Silvia says you've met my brother Phillip a few times too. So now you already know three of the seven of us. The rest are great."

He chews and then takes a sip of water. "Yeah. Phillip visits the city a lot. Silvia insisted I meet him. Bit uppity for me."

"He works with poor communities to bring them clean water. He's not really uppity. He's the UN Ambassador for Clean Water."

Dylan looks unimpressed. "A position they give to famous faces. He's the spare heir, isn't he?"

"He was before the new heiress was born. Gabriel has a one-year-old daughter now. Mila."

He goes back to eating. Finally he says, "There you go."

Maybe I'll work on a reconciliation from my family's side first. See if maybe Gabriel can make some headway. Dylan reminds me of Gabriel a bit in looks and manner, direct and authoritative.

I get back to my original purpose. "My friend is running a poker game here in Brooklyn, and I was hoping you might know something about some local Russians playing in the game."

"Why?"

"Because I want to make sure they're legit."

He takes a long drink of water. "There's a large Russian community over in the Brighton Beach area. Good people, very family oriented. I mean, yeah, the Russian mafia is there, but there's plenty of good folks too."

"I don't think they're from there. They're new immigrants with accents. Really wealthy, young, living in the Park Slope area, and I don't know where else."

He lifts a brow. "You got names?"

"Just a few."

"Well, gimme."

"I only know two. Sergei Rivkin and Yuri Petrov."

"Don't know Sergei. Now Yuri. If that's who I think it is, his dad's a big-time real estate developer."

"Yes, he mentioned that."

He shakes his head. "My uncle told us never to work for his projects. His dad gets into ridiculous debt, gambles with other people's money, and then doesn't pay his contractors. He puts good people out of business. I'd stay away from that one."

"He asked all of us to buy into a deal in Queens."

"Wouldn't recommend it."

"Sergei already put in some money. Like right away."

"If Sergei's connected to the mob, it could be a way to clean his money. If not, he made a really bad investment."

I watch as he finishes his sandwich in a few bites and then drains his water. He wipes his mouth on a napkin and gathers his trash on a tray. I get the feeling he's about to leave.

"Thanks for meeting me, Dylan. I was hoping to meet the rest of your family while I'm here too. I'd really like to connect again."

His expression is stone. "You met me. That's enough."

"But we're family. Don't you think they'd want to meet me?"

He presses his lips together. "No, I don't. It'll only hurt them." His blue eyes narrow. "You think we don't know what you think of us? My father told us. He was thrown out and told that he and his riffraff family could stay in Brooklyn forever exiled. No wealth or privilege that comes with his title, not even an allowance. You think it's easy for a man raised to the throne to make a living starting from scratch here?"

"What did he do?"

"He did what he had to. My uncle offered him a job in construction, asking him to keep the books. He's the office guy and worked like hell to learn everything he could about the business. My brothers and I joined them as soon as we were old enough. Byrne Construction is a family business. The Byrnes are my family, my mother's side. Not yours."

"I'm really sorry for the way things went down back then, but we're the new generation. We can make it right. The Rourkes are your family too."

He scowls. "You don't get it. I would've been king down the line. Instead, I'm here working hard labor while you're enjoying the good life up at the palace. Look, I came today out of respect for Silvia. I like her. That's enough Rourke family time for me."

"Will you come to dinner tonight at her place?"

He stands. "I'm beat, so I'll pass." He sets his dishes in the bin on top of the trash can and tosses his trash inside the can. "Gotta go."

I stand and cross to him. "There doesn't have to be so much bitterness between our families."

He tilts his head. "Doesn't have to be, but there is, and we both know whose fault that is. I'll let you know if anything turns up about Sergei. If you don't hear from me, it's all good."

"Can you tell your father I'd like to meet him?"

His jaw clenches just like Gabriel's does when he's irritated. "No."

"Why not?"

He speaks through his teeth. "He's suffered enough."

He strides out the door.

I go back to my table and sit with my espresso, lost in thought. Even though he was clearly not thrilled to spend time with me, he was helpful. And he did say he'd get back to me if there was a problem. If he was completely closed off from my family, he wouldn't even meet with me.

I look to the ceiling and blow out a sharp breath. There's reason to hope. Plus Silvia has met him and his brothers. Maybe Silvia is the key to uniting the families.

~

Sara

I don't think I've been this social in years. Drinks with both Rourke twins and now a dinner party at Silvia's apartment. I stopped uptown at Columbia to meet Chloe, and we rode the subway down to Central Park south, where Silvia and her husband live. It's pricey real estate, but not as upscale as I would've expected from royalty. I thought Silvia would buy a multimillion-dollar unit in the Dakota, where all the famous wealthy live. I did hear that Villroy's fishing economy was faltering and they bolstered it by using their fishing industry to make high-end cosmetics. The day spa and casino were created to pamper and entertain respectively, but it all started with cosmetics.

Chloe has barely spoken to me the whole way here because she's studying for an organic chemistry test through notes on her phone. I worry about this girl. I mean, she already did the hard part—got into the college she wanted and placed out of several intro science courses. Now that she's there, she needs to let loose a little.

I glance over at her. She's wearing her usual uniform of cardigan, tank top, and jeans. It's an all-weather foolproof system. Sometimes the cardigan comes off, and sometimes it stays on. Wow! The colors are a neutral palette that she mixes and matches. Today it's a pink cardigan over a light beige tank. She doesn't waste time on fashion. We resemble each other—same blond hair and green eyes—only she's petite with fine cheekbones and a bow to her top lip that makes her look like a sweet angel. She used to be hell on wheels. Now she's all study all the time.

"Okay, put your phone away," I tell her with a jab to the ribs.

Her eyes flash. "Ow!"

"Stop studying. We're going in the building now."

She sticks her phone in her purse. "You didn't have to jab me!"

"Yes, I did, because you don't hear me otherwise." I'm the mom, except I'm her big sister.

She gets quiet, and I see she's mouthing words to herself. She's not one for mocking backtalk. She's probably reciting scientific formulas.

I snap my fingers in front of her face to break the formula trance. "How's school?"

"Fantastic! My advisor worked out the perfect schedule for me to double major in bio and chem and still graduate in three years."

"Double major in three years? Why don't you just do the combined biochem?"

A serene smile blooms on her face. "Because there's so many courses I want to take in both bio and chem. I need the double major."

We stop at the front desk and check in. This place used to be a hotel and is now apartments.

"Silvia says she'll be down in a minute," the clerk says.

"Thank you." I turn to Chloe. "Have you been to any parties yet?"

"You know I'm not into the party scene. It's a waste of time."

"Are you making friends? Hanging out?" It's been a little over three weeks since she started school and I fear she's studying all the time.

"I do have a study group. About five of us, sometimes four."

"Anyone cute?"

She rolls her eyes. "I'm not looking for a boyfriend. I'm very focused on my goals right now. Three years and then I've got Harvard Medical School in my sights."

And then she'll be locked away in a lab for her career. "Maybe you could join a club."

"They do have a tutoring club to help underprivileged high school students."

I nearly smack my forehead because she's just not getting it. Not that there's anything wrong with a club like that. She was an underprivileged high school student not so long ago. I just want her to meet people her age socially.

She goes on. "I plan to volunteer at the hospital too. That starts next month."

Maybe she'll meet a doctor. That wouldn't be so bad since she wants to be a doctor too. I just want her to have a relatively normal college experience—friends, boyfriends, maybe the occasional rowdy night. The kind of experience I never got to have. I want everything for her.

"You're here!" a feminine voice exclaims.

We both turn to see Silvia beaming at us. "Thanks for coming on such short notice!" She hugs me and turns to Chloe. "Look at you! All grown up!" She hugs her, and Chloe gives her a stiff hug in return.

Silvia pulls back. "Do you remember me? You were only five the last time I saw you."

Chloe squints. "Vaguely. I remember the beach, and you had a white tent you sat under for a long time with a pile of books."

Silvia smiles. "And I helped you build sandcastles too, which you destroyed." She gestures for us to follow, her high ponytail swinging as she walks. She's wearing a pale pink silk blouse with dark gray trousers and black suede ankle-length boots. I'm glad I dressed up a bit in a green V-neck short-sleeved sweater, black jeans, and black ballet flats. Normally I'm in a T-shirt and shorts or jeans, unless I'm working. "This way to the elevator."

We follow her.

"My brother Adrian will be here soon," Silvia says to Chloe. "Do you remember him? He's my twin."

Chloe lifts one shoulder. "Also very vague. He played cards with Sara."

"And still does, right, Sara?" Silvia asks. "He told me he joined you for poker night."

"More like invited himself," I mutter.

Silvia laughs. "He could never pass up a good poker

game. He hasn't gotten to play as much now that he runs the casino." She smiles at us both. "This is so great. I can't believe I get to see you both after all these years."

The elevator doors open on the top floor, and we follow her to a corner apartment. The first thing I see is a wall of windows facing Central Park. The living room is large and has a desk by the window with a laptop and a seating area with a brown suede sofa and two turquoise chairs arranged around a glass coffee table. Across from that is a dining area with a black wood table and six matching wooden chairs.

A mountain of a man steps out of the adjacent kitchen. He's got a full beard, his dirty blond hair tied back in a low ponytail, tall and bulky with muscle. I'd almost say hipster territory, but he looks too much like a lumberjack. He doesn't look like the kind of man I pictured Silvia would choose. I thought for sure she'd want a fellow bookworm—a clean-shaven, neat hair part, academic type.

Silvia hooks her arm in his. "Cade, I'd like you to meet my oldest, dearest friends, Sara and Chloe. This is Cade."

My throat tightens unexpectedly. Silvia thinks of me as a dear friend? And I haven't stayed in touch. I feel horrible. My defenses were up, working overtime to prevent any more pain from coming my way with reminders of Villroy and my parents. I hope I haven't caused her pain in protecting myself.

Cade smiles and gives us both warm handshakes. "Great to meet you. I didn't have much notice, so we're having roast chicken, potatoes, and kale. Are either of you vegetarian?"

"No," I say.

"I'm thinking of trying it out," Chloe says thoughtfully. "But I'll wait until after our dinner."

I stare at her. That's new. She never told me that. She usually tells me everything.

"I tried it for a year in college," Cade says. "Couldn't stick to it. I only buy free-pasture meat, so it's better for you and the animal."

Silvia wraps her arms around his middle and gives him a squeeze. "Cade's the chef around here. I clean up the mess."

He gives her a kiss. "I'd better go check on dinner." He disappears into the kitchen.

I head over to the view of Central Park, peeking into the kitchen on my way. It's a small kitchen but modern with stainless steel appliances and dark wood cabinetry. I wonder about the rent but don't ask. I'm sure it's a lot more than I could afford.

"I got us some champagne to celebrate our reunion," Silvia says, bringing the bottle and some glasses over to the coffee table. "I'll wait for Adrian to get here to do our toast."

The intercom buzzes.

She gestures toward it. "Speak of the devil and he arrives!" She calls downstairs to let him up. I guess he knows his way. She turns back to us. "Oh, Chloe, would you like sparkling water instead? I forgot you're not legal yet."

"One glass won't hurt her," I say.

"I'd prefer water," Chloe says. "I'm going to be studying later tonight and need a clear head."

Silvia smiles. "Sara told me you're a star student. You're going to be a doctor, right?"

"Yes," Chloe says. "I want to be a medical researcher. I plan to cure cancer." She says it matter-of-factly, not in the least bit braggy, her expression dead serious.

Silvia glances at me, her lips curving into a small smile, before turning back to Chloe. "Very impressive."

"I'm not trying to impress," Chloe says. "I'm trying to improve humanity."

"Well, somebody has to," Silvia says with a laugh.

Chloe doesn't laugh. She's not one for joking or silliness of any kind. That playful side of her died with our parents. I can't blame her, but I'd hoped she'd reclaim it in college.

There's a knock at the door, and I turn as Silvia answers it. Adrian and his guard, Jack, are standing there. Jack remains in the hall while Adrian walks in, giving his sister a hug, his gaze meeting mine over her shoulder. I flush with heat. That's never happened to me before with just a look.

He crosses to me, leans down and kisses my cheek. "I need to talk to you later."

I'm instantly wary. He's been poking around my game. If there's any bad news about the guys, I don't want to know. He doesn't wait for my response, instead turning to greet Chloe warmly.

"I remember you like this," he says, holding his hand down at belly-button level to show how small she was. "Now you're on your way to being a doctor."

"That's right," she says.

"How's Columbia?" he asks.

Chloe launches into a detailed description of her professors and classes. Adrian listens attentively, which I give him a lot of credit for because it's not always easy to follow what she's studying.

When Chloe finally winds down, Silvia tells us to gather around the coffee table for a toast. "You too, Cade!" she calls. "Oh, bring the Pellegrino too."

We all gather around, and Silvia pours the champagne and a glass of sparkling water for Chloe. She holds up her glass and waits for us all to lift ours.

Silvia takes us all in. "I just want to say that I'm so, so glad we can all be together once again, and I hope this is just the beginning of a continued wonderful friendship. To Sara and Chloe!"

"To Sara and Chloe," Adrian echoes with a warm smile.

A pang of guilt hits me. They're being so nice to us. I definitely should've gotten in touch sooner.

We all clink glasses and drink. Chloe looks a little lost. She barely remembers them. I do, though, and it means a lot.

"Dinner will be in five minutes," Cade says.

"Let's take this over to the dining room table," Silvia says, heading over there with her drink.

Adrian pulls out a chair and gestures for me to take it. More gentleman manners. I can't help my smile. "Do they teach you that at prince training school?"

He pushes my chair in after I'm seated. "I definitely suffered through my share of etiquette lessons." He goes to help Chloe into her chair, but she promptly sits down on her own. I don't think she even noticed his effort.

Adrian takes the seat across from me and turns to Silvia. "Speaking of suffering and reunions, I met with Dylan earlier." He turns to me and Chloe. "That's my cousin from the side of the family that was exiled."

"How did it go?" Silvia asks. "Isn't he a gruff and growly sweetheart?"

Adrian presses his lips together. "He was gruff all right, but he did meet with me and was helpful. Anyway, he wasn't too keen on a family reunion, but I think it's time. With Gabriel and Anna ruling, I think we could lift the exile and welcome them back to Villroy."

"But would they want to go back?" Silvia asks. "I've met Dylan and his brothers, and they were friendly enough, but any time I mentioned home, they sounded bitter."

"All the more reason to bring them back into the fold."

"You could try."

"*You* could try. Dylan thinks highly of you. I think you could be the sweetness that balances out all the sour that went before."

She smiles and says conspiratorially to me and Chloe, "My brother has a very high opinion of me."

"It has to be you," Adrian says.

She tilts her head. "I'll try. I have to clear it first with Gabriel and Anna."

"You know Gabriel would do anything for you."

"Okay, okay!" Silvia exclaims. "What a bossy pants you've turned into since becoming the boss at the casino." She says it with great affection, clearly proud of her brother.

"Speaking of," Adrian says, turning to me. "Have you given any thought to flying back with me to check out the casino? I'd love your opinion on the running of the place."

I go cold, chest tight. *Breathe!* The truth is, I'm afraid all of the grief will come flooding back, but I can't admit I'm too scared to face it. I want him to think I'm strong, capable, and completely past this. They died twelve years ago. It shouldn't have such a stranglehold on me. I swallow hard.

"Sara?" Adrian prompts.

I glance at Chloe and realize I have a perfectly legitimate

reason not to go—she needs me. "I can't. Chloe's here. She just started school."

Chloe's brows lift. I send her a sharply worded telepathic message: *It's true! You're my responsibility. I'm your legal guardian.*

"Just for a short visit," Adrian says. "Doesn't Chloe live in a dorm now?"

"Yes." Chloe turns to me. "I'm fine if you go away for a few days. Actually, I'm fine even if you wanted to stay longer." She tucks her hair behind her ears, pink dotting her cheeks. "I'm not a kid anymore, Sara."

I've embarrassed her. "I know that. But what if you need something? And what about our weekly dinner?"

Chloe enunciates slowly and clearly, "I'll. Be. Fine."

Now I'm the one who's embarrassed. My cheeks burn. It almost seems like she doesn't need me anymore. How could this be? Chloe has depended on me for absolutely everything since she was six years old. It hurts more than I thought possible, a hollow, empty ache in my chest. The one tie I kept in my life is cutting herself loose. I stare at the table, mentally reviewing all the ways I've been there for her—helping her study, cooking for her (or bringing her my portion of food), being her confidante, going with her to the doctor and the dentist, paying our bills, buying her anything she needed.

My wretched discovery of my nonessential part in her life is interrupted by the arrival of dinner. I can barely focus on the food. Chloe outgrew me. I mean, I knew she would eventually, I wanted her to, but not yet. When she was in medical school, or maybe in her senior year of college. Not now, three weeks into her first semester. Is this why she's been so quiet tonight?

I glance over as she eats her meal with her usual studied intensity; her mind is probably back on her organic chem exam. When I wasn't looking, she moved on. Now what am I supposed to do? Who do I pour all my love and care into? There's no one else in the world I trust enough to open up with.

Maybe I should get a pet. *No-o-o.* It's not the same. I want my little sister back.

Dinner passes in a blur. Silvia keeps up enough conversation for everyone.

I just keep watching Chloe. Is she happy? Did I do enough for her? Is she really ready to be on her own without me?

I think I failed her. I taught her to work hard, but I forgot to teach her to enjoy herself. But maybe her studies are what make her happy. I'd just like to see some joy from her once in a while. I haven't seen jubilance from her since we were last on Villroy. Would Villroy bring some of the old Chloe back?

I'm being silly. There's nothing magical about Villroy. It certainly wouldn't bring anything back for me but grief.

As soon as we finish dessert, Chloe pipes up. "Thanks for a great meal. Much better than the caf, but I need to get back. I still have a lot of studying to do." She stands abruptly, in a hurry to get back.

"Time for an all-nighter, eh?" Silvia asks. "I remember those."

Chloe stares at her. "I never pull an all-nighter. I schedule my time exactly right to prevent that. It's unhealthy to stay up all night, and you retain little when you're sleep deprived."

"Smart girl," Silvia says. "Now I see why you're the doctor."

"You want a lift?" Adrian asks Chloe, rising from his seat. "My driver is here. I can take you both home." He looks over at me.

"I'm out of the way in Brooklyn," I say, standing and hooking my purse strap over my shoulder. "I'll just take the train."

"Oh, come on," Silvia says. "You'd rather ride public transit than ride with Adrian? Oops. Are you two on the outs?"

I blush, even though nothing happened. It's what I'm afraid is going to happen if I keep spending time with him just the two of us. There's too much chemistry, which makes it too risky to get close to him. At the same time, it would be an insult at this point to turn his offer down.

I paste on a smile as Adrian closes the distance between us, my cheeks and neck heating. "I'd be happy for a ride. Thank you."

Adrian squeezes my shoulder as he leans close. "Good," he growls in my ear. "Because you were coming with me anyway."

I shoot him a hard look, trying to cover my reaction to that commanding voice. My skin prickles with goose bumps, my pulse scrambling. "You are a bossy pants." And as independent as I am, I like it way too much.

He winks. "Mr. Bossy Pants to you." His gaze drops to my forearm, where goose bumps give me away. He smirks, and my cheeks flame.

A few minutes later, we say our goodbyes and head downstairs to his car with his guard. Adrian called ahead and had his driver bring the car around. The three of us pile into the backseat with me in the middle between Chloe and Adrian. It's roomy enough I'm not squished, but I'm definitely aware of how close Adrian is, his spicy scent washing over me. The heat of his body makes me want to press close and inhale him. I don't think I can resist him much longer.

Chloe pulls her phone out and starts studying. I can see the complex equations on the screen. If only she was texting a friend or playing a stupid game, anything would be better than constant studying. I definitely failed her and now it's too late. I'm at a loss on how to fix it, so I focus on something else.

I turn to Adrian. "You mentioned you wanted to talk to me about something earlier. What was it?"

He glances meaningfully toward Chloe.

"She's studying, tuning out the world."

He keeps his voice low. "I asked my cousin about Yuri's land deal—he knows a lot of people in construction—and he says it's no good. Yuri's father, who runs the company, doesn't pay his contractors and gambles away his money. He's in serious debt on his projects. Seems like a shady guy."

I take this in for a moment, and then realize he's asking around about my players. "Why were you asking about my players' business? They're just having fun and enjoying themselves. Besides, I screened ahead of time to be sure no one was involved in drugs, human trafficking, or anything like that. I have standards. What they do in their business doesn't concern me."

"If they all go in on this, they may lose so much money they won't be your players anymore. And you should care what they do. They could be connected to the Russian mafia."

I shake my head. "Now you're being ridiculous. They're nice guys."

"To *you* they're nice. My cousin says the Russian mafia is alive and well here."

I lift a shoulder in a careless shrug. My players seem like men everywhere, looking out for themselves and taking what they want. And what they want is a good poker game.

"Would you care if they were?" he asks.

I clamp my mouth shut, tired of him poking around in my business.

His voice is a fierce growl. "Sara."

My body responds with a lusty roar to life—my nerve endings tingling, my stomach doing a flip, and a low ache of need. Dammit.

I turn away, focusing on my sister instead. "Chloe." No response. "Chloe!" I cover her phone with my hand.

She looks up, blinking like she just came out of a trance. "Huh?"

"Do you need any money? Any clothes or shoes? Anything?"

She goes back to her phone, muttering, "I'm fine."

I look out the window, my throat tight. She's been the center of my life, my purpose for so long. I can't quite believe she doesn't need me anymore.

When we arrive at her dorm, I get out of the car, hug her, and slip a twenty into her pocket. "I love you. Please make time for something fun for you."

She sticks her hand in her pocket and pulls the money out. "Sara! I said I'm fine." She tries to hand it back, but I push it toward her.

"Promise me you'll have some fun."

"Working at the hospital is fun."

"Okay, and then maybe have a beer or something after a shift with some coworkers."

She frowns. "You have to be twenty-one to drink."

How did I raise such a rule follower? I swear I wasn't that hard on her. "Have a soda, then, I don't care. Just don't be all study all the time."

She looks puzzled for a moment, like I'm changing the programming she's used to.

I press on. "You're in college now, young and on your own in the city. Have some fun."

"You should go to Villroy with Adrian."

Before I can explain all the reasons why that's a terrible idea—my poker game here, the wrenching memories of our parents, my need to keep a safe distance from Adrian—she gives me a quick squeeze and races back to her dorm.

I get back in the car, bereft.

"What's wrong?" Adrian asks.

I gesture out the window toward her dorm. "What was all this for, if she's just going to waste her college years studying?"

He gives me a strange look. "Don't you want her to study?"

"Yes! But I want her to enjoy herself too."

"Like you."

It hits me then that she doesn't know how to enjoy herself because I never showed her. I worked hard, so she worked hard too. I should've balanced it out better to teach her by example. The regret tastes bitter in my mouth. Just add that to my list of regrets. I regret not keeping in touch with Silvia, too, my dear friend. I regret losing Adrian, the sweet boy who was once my hero. Now he's a bossy man who sticks his nose in my business far too much. I don't need someone telling me what to do. That's my job.

I go on the defensive because I'm near my breaking point, and I do *not* want to cry in front of him. "Hey, this isn't about me. I do what I want when I want."

"Maybe she does too," he says mildly.

"I've failed her," I whisper over the lump in my throat. "And now it's too late. She's all grown up and moved on." A voice in my head taunts me: *everyone you love leaves you.* My eyes are hot; my gut knots. I hate this.

"C'mere," he says and puts his arm around me, hauling me against his shoulder.

It feels so good I don't protest. No one ever holds me.

"You haven't failed her," he says. "She's doing fantastic. She's smart, capable, and doing what she loves. She's so enthusiastic about all of her classes and becoming a doctor. There's nothing wrong with that."

"She's missing out on the college experience."

"This is her college experience, done her way."

He strokes my hair back from my face, and the warmth and tenderness of the gesture undoes me.

I look up at him, and the pull to close the distance overwhelms me. I need to be close. I press my lips to his. A shock ripples through me. *Yes. This is exactly what I need, to lose myself in sensation and not think about my regrets.*

I kiss him again, harder this time, and he nips my lower lip in retaliation. The kiss turns wild, hot, carnal. There's no mistaking where this is going. His hands are all over me. I'm burning up, dying to climb into his lap, but I need more than I can get away with in a car.

I tear my mouth away. "Spend the night with me."

His eyes burn into mine. "We'll go to my hotel." He brushes his thumb over my lower lip and pushes past my teeth into my mouth. I suck his finger, and he groans.

He barks out the new destination to the driver. We're really doing this. My heart thunders in my chest.

He turns back to me and frames my face with both hands and kisses me once more gently. "Sara."

That's all. One word said with so much affection, warmth, and desire. I melt despite my usually tough shell.

"Adrian," I say on a sigh.

And there are no more words. An understanding passes between us. It was always going to come to this. As inevitable as the sun setting, or our reunion. We had a pact.

8

Adrian

I have the penthouse suite, which means a private elevator. My guard goes to his room on the floor below me, and I take Sara's hand, entwining our fingers together, as we ride up to my suite. This moment feels inevitable, like we were always meant to come together in this way. We just had to reach the magic age of twenty-five for everything to click into place. It was in the cards—our younger selves knew.

She gives me a sideways look. "I should've known you'd have the penthouse suite." Her voice sounds tight. Is she nervous?

I give her hand a squeeze. "There are perks to being a prince. Doesn't mean I always get what I want."

She sends me an incredulous look. "What have you ever *not* gotten that you wanted?"

"You."

Pink blooms on her cheeks, and she gets quiet for a moment. "Well, you can have me tonight."

"I definitely will." And after that, too, I add silently. I don't kiss her, even though I'm dying to. My need is too great, and I don't want elevator sex, or living-room-sofa sex. I want her in a big bed, where I can take my time with her.

The elevator doors open directly into my suite, which

takes up the entire top floor. I scoop her up into my arms, and she squeals. "What are you doing?"

I cross through the living room. "Carrying you to my bed."

Her green eyes are huge, her cheeks and neck pink. "You're a secret romantic, aren't you?"

"Actually, I'm extremely practical. Fastest way to get you to bed is to carry you. See? Here we are." I set her down in the center of the king-size bed.

She throws her arms and legs to the sides. "Oh my God, it's like a big fluffy cloud!"

"Goose down." I unbutton my shirt as she watches.

She props up on her elbows. "Is this weird? The two of us getting naked after being friends for so long? I mean, we knew each other best as kids."

I jerk my chin at her. "Take off your shirt, and I'll let you know."

She pulls off her V-neck shirt and tosses it to the side. Lust surges through me. She's mouthwatering, her full breasts in a lacy pink bra. "Well?" she asks.

There's still her black jeans and shoes, but this is such a good view I can't wait.

I kiss her, covering her with my body. Her arms wrap around my neck, her legs spreading to cradle me close. Perfection. I kiss and caress as I strip her down, loving every-thing I see and feel and taste. She's smooth, soft, and tastes like vanilla. I cannot get enough.

She shoves the covers away so she's lying on the silk sheets and lets out a soft sigh. She appreciates the luxury of the bed, and I appreciate her being naked in it. I lower myself down her body, kissing as I go.

"Adrian," she says, her fingers running through my hair, "it's been so long for me. Now." She tugs my hair. "I don't want to wait."

I've barely gotten started. I rise up over her, grab her hands, and pin them to the bed. I lower my voice to the deep growl that gives her goose bumps. "Turns out I'm in charge."

She shivers, her eyes dilating. "I *love* that growly voice."

I smile. "I know. Now say my name when you come."

"Oh, that doesn't always..." She trails off because I've slipped a hand between us, stroking her.

Within minutes, she's moaning. And then I do one better and slide down her body, putting my mouth to work where my fingers left off. Her hips arch, seeking more, and I give her what she needs, sliding my fingers inside her and stroking her on the inside. She cries out, bucking wildly, and then her entire body shudders as she comes into my mouth. Fucking amazing. I'm so turned on.

I lift my head. She collapses into the mattress, breathing hard, her eyes wide open, staring at the ceiling.

I kiss my way back up her body and grin. "You forgot to say my name." I kiss her. "Say my name."

"Adrian," she whispers, her fingers sliding into my hair, her gaze focusing on me. "Amazing Adrian."

"Ready for more?"

She nods. "I ache for you."

I groan, get out of bed, and grab a condom from the nightstand. I always have some just in case. I roll it on and turn back to her.

She's on all fours and looks at me over her shoulder. "Fuck me."

My cock surges, and I don't waste time, grabbing her by the hips and thrusting deep. She gasps, and I groan. I can't go slow. It's intense throbbing heat. Her body squeezes me rhythmically; she's already going over again. I slip my fingers between her legs, and she drops her head, saying my name in a chant that fills my mind. I want to possess her. I want her to always say my name.

She stiffens and then she goes off, rocking under me. I let go, thrusting deep over and over. Sensation explodes through me in a fiery burst.

Jesus. It's never been that intense before.

I run a hand up her spine and give the back of her neck a squeeze. She practically purrs, her cheek turning into the pillow, her lips curving up in a smile.

I pull out and lie down beside her, stroking her back.

She turns her head to face me. "Awesome."

I can't help my smile. It was awesome. "Next time I want to see your face."

"I like it better with you behind me."

"Why?"

"I guess because it's just about sensation, not, you know, checking in with each other. Basic and primal."

I kiss her. "Nothing wrong with primal, but I want to see your expression when you lose your mind."

"Someone's confident."

I roll her to her side and pull her close, tucking my leg between hers and applying just enough pressure to get her attention.

She moans. "Wicked man."

I stroke her soft blond hair back from her face. "Sara, this isn't a onetime thing. You know that, right?"

"You want to talk about the relationship? Seriously?"

I nip her lip for mocking me, and she responds with a wild passionate kiss in return. Did not expect that, but I go with it. Impossible not to. She tries to climb on top of me, so I roll to my back and let her, spreading her legs over me.

"Look what you made me do," she says with a bright smile. "I want you again."

I hold her face in my hands, sensing she's avoiding the intensity of what we have. "I'm not asking for promises, but this right here, you and me, is not your standard one-night thing. We have a history. You're a part of me, just like I'm a part of you. It's good, really good. I'm not letting you go so easily this time."

She stares at me for a moment before her expression shutters closed. She's got a killer shield around her heart. I'm not sure she lets anyone in ever, but she can trust me.

"Sara."

She climbs off me and flops onto her back, nearly vibrating with tension. I pull the covers over us both, and then I wait. I sense she's trying to decide if she'll stay with me for whatever this thing is between us, or retreat to her defensive self. I'm starting to learn her ways.

Finally, she stares at the ceiling and says, "I don't do long term, and I don't do relationships. It's nothing personal. I just…can't."

I prop up on one elbow to look into her eyes, where she's lying on her back. "Are you telling me you've never had a relationship?"

Her chin juts out. "That's right. By my choice."

"Relationships are a bad bet."

She relaxes. "Yes! If you think the same way, then we can just enjoy each other."

"I did think that way for a long time, but maybe I was just waiting for you."

"Adrian," she says in a choked voice, her eyes welling.

"We were close, and it killed me not to have you in my life. I always thought of you, always hoped you were okay. Why didn't you keep in touch? Silvia and I both tried to connect with you."

"I'm sorry," she says, blinking tears away. "I couldn't. You were all tied up with memories of my summers on Villroy with my parents, and I couldn't go there. It would've left me heartbroken, and I needed to be strong to be there for Chloe."

I kiss her. "Silvia suspected she and I were tied up with your Villroy memories."

She strokes my hair. "Now that I've seen you both again, I regret letting so much time pass."

I nuzzle her neck and breathe her in. "No regrets. We'll make new memories now, here. More than one night. I can't say goodbye to you so soon."

"As long as you're in town. You leave Friday, right?"

"Yes." And I want to bring you back with me, I add silently. It's Wednesday night, which means she's granting me two more days. I need more time.

I can't leave Villroy. They're counting on me to make the casino a success and give our economy that final push it needs to be sustainable long term. For the first time in my life, my kingdom needs me, and I won't let Villroy down. This is my legacy, and I want Sara to be part of it. I know she couldn't handle Villroy memories when she was younger, but this Sara—as strong and capable as she is—can definitely handle it. She can visit her sister. Chloe doesn't need her as much now that she's an adult.

She smiles, looking relieved. "Okay, we have until Friday, and then we'll keep in touch."

It's not enough.

"Okay?" she presses, practically begging me to go along. Obviously she needs more time.

"Okay."

She cuddles up against me and sighs.

There's no question in my mind that there is a future for us. I feel like I've waited my whole life for her. She's not ready to hear that now. I need to choose my moment.

~

Sara

Adrian stayed two weeks more than he planned, and I'm okay with it. More than okay. He was right about us. It feels easy, like we picked up where we left off, not heavy like a relationship. He's leaving tomorrow, and I'll truly miss him. I hope he'll visit regularly. Him being the boss and having access to a private jet makes that a real possibility. This is the kind of tie I can handle. There're natural boundaries that keep it a casual thing.

It's late afternoon on Thursday, and I have to get ready for tonight's poker game. We're going to be at this funky hotel in an artsy neighborhood across town. I arranged for a suite and ordered some food from a Jewish neighborhood—cheese blintzes and rugelach—and lots of fresh fruit. It's important that I change things up so there's always a nice surprise when the guys show up to the game.

Adrian is poking around my studio apartment. We've spent most of our time at his hotel or in the city. "You *and* Chloe lived here?"

I laugh. "I know it's tiny, but we had a system. Everything

worked out ahead of time, from sharing the bathroom to meals. She made breakfast, and I made dinner or brought home dinner from the diner. We shared the futon. It pulls out to a queen-size bed."

He stares at the futon, which is looking kind of old, then looks at me. "It must be hard to be here by yourself after being so close to your sister."

I'm shocked at his insight. "Yes. It's been hard. I've never lived alone." My throat tightens. "It's like I lost the best part of me."

He nods. "It was similar when Silvia and I separated to go to different universities. Twins have an extra close bond from sharing the womb. She went to Yale here in the US, and I went to Cambridge in England. We'd never been so far away from each other before. Of course, we kept in touch and visited, but it wasn't the same. The twin bond is still there, but it stretched, you know, letting other people in between us. She has Cade now."

I step closer, drawn by his openness. Most men don't share like this with me. "You seem as close as ever to me."

His hazel eyes are direct. "We're close, it's just different. Sort of like you and Chloe. She's changing into the woman she's meant to become and moving into the next part of her life."

I hug him, an unusual gesture for me. It's just so good to have someone really understand what I'm going through, separating from Chloe.

He kisses my hair. "I got it right what's going on with you."

I press my cheek to his chest, listening to the steady thump of his heart. "Yes."

His voice rumbles in his chest. "Having a female twin gives me unique insight into the female mind."

A surge of affection rushes through me, and I kiss him, and then I kiss him again and again. The fire ignites once more, and we rip each other's clothes off.

Next thing I know, he's lifting me right up against the wall. I wrap my legs around him, hanging on as he pounds into me, his mouth on my neck, sucking hard. My head arches back, my eyes closing, consumed by the fire between us. His fingers slip between us, adding another level of intensity. I'm panting, sensation clouding my mind, the pleasure overwhelming me. His mouth claims mine, and I explode, a starburst of pleasure shooting through my entire body. He thrusts more and more, and I never want him to stop. I go over again, shuddering with my release, and this time he goes with me, his lips pressed against the side of my neck.

We stay like that for long moments, plastered together, breathing hard. We are animals—primal and basic. No messy emotions that hurt and betray with their temporary nature. Just raw sensation. It's exactly what I want.

He lifts his head and stares at my neck. "I marked you."

I put a hand to my neck, alarmed. "You gave me a hickey?"

He brushes my hand away and runs his finger over my neck. "I got you good." He sounds pleased.

"Adrian! I'm seeing the guys tonight. How bad is it? Can I cover it with makeup?"

"Leave it," he growls in a command that my body responds to instantly. Desire pools between my legs, soaking him, where he's still buried deep inside me. My lips part. I'm caught in sensations that overwhelm any rational thought.

His lips curve, his eyes knowing. "You are *perfect* for me."

I'm speechless and shockingly eager for more of the pleasure he gives.

He lifts me off him and sets me on my feet, holding me by the arms to steady me. My legs are so wobbly.

I finally find my voice. "Is this hickey an alpha-dog thing? You want them to know I was with you?"

He holds my jaw with one hand, his eyes intent on mine. "I want everyone to know you're mine. It's not alpha dog. It's a fact. I claimed you."

I get hotter and wetter by his hold on me, his words, his heated eyes. I want to protest that I'm not his, but part of me wants to be possessed by him. "Yes."

He groans, his mouth covering mine, his tongue thrusting

inside. Adrian claims me, and I surrender to the passion I've never experienced before him. I can enjoy this knowing we understand each other, just a temporary insanely passionate time before he goes back home.

9

Adrian

Sara is in the shower, getting ready for the game. I'd join her in there if it wasn't so tiny. I don't even think I could turn around without knocking my elbows into the sides. I look around her place. There's one tiny closet. Inside is her small wheeled suitcase, where she keeps the stuff for the game, including the lockbox for the money. She either needs a guard or a better, less risky job. Like, say, working at my casino. First I have to get her to agree to a visit.

I prolonged my stay here, wanting to be with her as long as I could, but I really need to get back to the casino. Emma keeps asking me when I'll be back, tired of taking my place. And I know her heart's not in it. I'm the one who can make the casino a success, and I want Sara by my side helping me do it. She says she's considering my job offer, but I can sense her reluctance. She's placating me, afraid to visit Villroy. I'm pretty sure it's that and not me that's the problem.

She emerges a short while later, wearing a dark green sleeveless turtleneck with black trousers. "The one thing I have that covers better than makeup." She shoots me a triumphant look.

I cross to her, folding the collar down to admire my love bite. "Where's the fun in that?"

She swats my hand away. "Don't be a Neanderthal."

"Why not? You like it."

Pink dots her cheeks. "In bed I like it. Not anywhere else."

I gesture toward where we just had sex. "Against the wall too."

She holds up a finger, a stern expression on her face. I grab her finger and nip it.

She plasters herself against me, her mouth colliding with mine, her fingers tunneling through my hair. *Jesus.* I'm rock hard, ready to have her again. I've never had a woman respond to me the way she does. She hikes her leg up, trying to climb me. I give her a boost, and she wraps her arms and legs around me, moaning into my mouth. We're zero to sixty in one bite.

I lower her to the futon and cover her, settling between her legs. Then I lift my head and grin. I can't help it. She wants me so badly she can barely keep her clothes on. "Let's get you out of these nice things."

She closes her eyes and groans. "What is wrong with me? I need to get over there to set up."

I kiss her. "You can't resist me."

"I'm not usually like this. Ever."

"You've been waiting for me." It's how I feel. I hope she feels the same.

Her eyes widen. "You're so arrogant."

I stroke her hair back and cup her cheek, serious now. "Just like I've been waiting for you. That's why we made a pact to marry when we turned twenty-five. That's why we found each other again. You and me. Meant to be, had to be, like the last card dealt. The only good bet."

She shoves at my chest. "I have to go."

I don't let her up because I need more. "Come back with me to Villroy tomorrow. I want you to see the casino." I kiss her and then gaze into her eyes, trying to show her how much this means to me. "I want you to consider working there. I want you to consider us."

She blinks rapidly, like she's trying not to cry. "Adrian," she whispers, "I can't."

She's scared of Villroy and maybe she's scared of what she feels for me. It's intense, I know, but nothing has ever felt more right.

I brush my lips over hers. "Just a visit. Just to see."

"No."

I get off her and pull her up to sit next to me. "Why not?"

"Why do I need a reason? I don't want to go."

I exhale sharply. "Is it Villroy or me?"

She crosses her arms, hugging herself. "Does it matter?"

"Yes. If it's Villroy, I can work with that. If it's me, then I'll leave you alone."

Her gaze shifts to the side, one of her tells. "It's you."

It's not me. She's just as into this thing between us as I am. I know it in my gut. She's afraid to see Villroy, just like she was afraid to get back in the water after she sliced her foot open in the ocean. But I stayed with her back then, played poker with her, kissed her, until she relaxed enough to enjoy the water again. I was her hero then, and I'll be her hero now.

"Okay," I say.

Her head whirls toward me in surprise. "Okay?"

"Mmm-hmm."

"You're not going to drag me there by the hair?"

I lower my voice to the deep growl that makes her wet. "More likely I'd gag and bind you, toss you over my shoulder, and put you on my private jet." Her cheeks flush pink, her eyes dilating. I can read her, and I love what I see. "But no. I respect your wishes."

Her face falls. "Oh. Thank you."

She sounds disappointed. Good. I don't leave until tomorrow, and I want her to go willingly. I just need to get her so comfortable with me that she can face her fear of seeing Villroy again. We'll make new memories there for however long she's willing to give me. I don't expect everything. Just a visit. Just a chance.

Taking a chance is what all good gamblers do, only this is the riskiest bet I've ever taken. I'm going all in on us.

Sara

I'm tempted by Adrian, I really am. And with the jet I could go to Villroy and be back in time for my Tuesday night poker game. Still, my intense fear of getting sucked under by grief has me digging my heels in. I mean, just thinking about my parents makes my chest ache. Half the time I forget to breathe. Actually seeing our cottage or the beach where we spent so much time, I'm afraid I'll fall apart. The panic attacks will take over. It took so long to put myself back together again. I told him no, and I'm sticking by it.

We're in the hotel suite I booked for the game now. I can feel him watching me as I set up the table with the card shuffler and chips.

"When's Gustavo get here?" he asks casually. That's my dealer.

I glance over at him. "Why?"

He waggles his brows.

I laugh, shaking my head. "We are not doing it here right before the game."

"There's a bedroom. Why not?"

I park a hand on my hip. "That's like your signature phrase, why not?"

"It's how I live my life. Want to try something? Why not? Go for it." He gestures toward the bedroom.

I shake my head, smiling. Then it hits me that he's fearless. He goes for what he wants when he wants it. "You're lucky to have that attitude. I'm sure being the youngest and a prince gave you a lot of confidence and support. I've only had me to lean on."

He closes the distance and pulls me into his arms. "Now you have me too." He presses my head to his chest. "Enjoy the lean."

I laugh, but then I wrap my arms around him and sigh. It's heaven to be held by Adrian. Warm, spicy, sexy heaven.

"Is it bad that I want you again?" he asks.

I smile up at him. "It's very flattering. And mutual, but we can't just be having sex all the time."

"Why—"

"Not," I finish for him. "See, I'm catching on." I pull away. "Because I've got things to do."

He gives my hair a tug. "Like me."

I laugh. "Incorrigible."

"Thank you."

By the time the guys arrive, I'm in a really good mood. Everything looks great, and I feel great, inside and out. That's Adrian's doing, I know.

I can feel his eyes on me as I greet my players. I catch his eye, and my breath stalls at the smoldering heat in them. I flush hot, losing my train of thought as I put the buy-in cash away with a smile plastered on my face. Who am I kidding with the casual thing? It's way too intense to be called casual.

The guys help themselves to the food and drink, taking shot glasses of vodka back with them to the table, where Gustavo is waiting to deal. Adrian takes Sergei's place at the table like he's been doing for the past several games. The guys like him. I'll have to go over my waiting list and find another player for Tuesday's game once Adrian leaves. My gut churns at the thought. I know it'll be hard to say goodbye, but I chose to let him close for a couple of weeks, so now I have to deal with the fallout. It's not goodbye forever, I reassure myself. We're going to keep in touch.

The guys start in with their usual banter, and I smile to myself, tucking away the lockbox of money and perching on a nearby chair, pretending to be on my phone while I keep my ears tuned to the play. Whenever they call out to me specifically, I'm always right there with a cheerful response. I really need this game to continue doing well. Covering Sergei's loss cleaned me out. Now I don't even have the money for Chloe's January tuition bill. Hopefully tonight someone will get on a roll and bring the pot high. Lately, the guys have been playing small. I'm not sure what's up. Is it because Sergei didn't return? Are they mad at me for kicking their friend out of the game? Maybe he's claiming he paid his debt and I had sour grapes. I can't get into all that with them. I'm Sunny Sara, the source of fun, not angst.

A few minutes later, Ivan asks Yuri about the Queens

project, and play stops dead while the men ask question after question. Shit. I think they all went in on it. I can only hope they didn't spend all their reserves to go all in the way Sergei did.

It's only midnight when Ivan folds. "That's all for me tonight."

No-o-o! The game usually goes much longer, and the guys play much looser the more it goes on.

"It's early," I say. "How about we add some Red Bull to that vodka?" Caffeine and vodka, the drink to keep you wide awake drunk. Except these guys never seem that affected by the vodka, just relaxed. Their tolerance is insane.

"Another time," Ivan says, rising from the table.

The other guys mutter similarly and, one by one, call it a night. I panic, about to do something crazy like offer to cover higher bets, when Adrian pipes up.

"Hey, you all should come to my casino on Villroy Island. I'm leaving tomorrow by private jet. Join me. I'll set you up with comps—free drinks, meals, and you can stay at the palace. You could jet over to nearby Monte Carlo to check out the casino there too. Lot of celebrities hang in both places. Ever hear of Jackson Walker? He performs at my casino."

The guys are psyched, talking over each other in their excitement.

"Jackson Walker!"

"He's a rock god."

"Legend."

Yuri even plays air guitar and rocks out, thrashing his head.

Adrian glances over at me. "Sara, you should come too, set everything up there for a cool poker game in a private room."

I nod once, my lips pressed tightly together. He forced my hand. I have to go. The guys will expect to see me there, and I need them to think I'm key to the fun, not some random casino person. I can't lose this game. Hell. Me on Villroy, the one place I hoped never to see again.

Adrian turns back to the group. "I'll have you back Sunday night."

"Hell yes!" Ivan exclaims. "I've always wanted to try my hand in Monte Carlo, and I'd like to see your place too."

"Great," Adrian says. "You're going to love it. There's a spa next door if you want a massage. That's comped too." He gives them his cell phone number and the address of the private airport in New Jersey, telling them the flight leaves at ten a.m. tomorrow. "We can get in a few hours of play Friday night in Villroy. You can stay in the palace guest rooms, spend Saturday on Villroy, and then jet over to Monte Carlo to play Saturday night."

The guys are thrilled, and I force myself to join in their enthusiasm. They take their leave in good spirits, clapping Adrian on the shoulder and thanking him. They tip me better than the last game.

As soon as everyone has cleared out, I sit on the sofa, lean forward, and drop my head in my hands. Part of me is thankful that Adrian salvaged a night that was rapidly going downhill after a series of less-than-stellar games. The other part is angry and scared. I *have* to go. I have to face the past I've tried so hard to move away from.

And what if the guys don't want to go back to my local game after having a taste of sophisticated European casinos?

Adrian sits next to me and rubs my back. "Are you angry I invited them?"

I lift my head. "I'm not sure."

"Then you're not."

I straighten. "You forced my hand. And are you really going to have them stay at the palace? I thought that was just for the royal family."

"We have guest rooms from when we were taking guests for honeymoons and ladies' weeks before the spa opened. We only let in people we're friends with. It's no problem. You'll be with me in my suite in the west wing. They'll be in the east wing."

I clench my hands tightly together. "I feel like I have to go. I don't like feeling forced into it."

"You don't have to go."

"Yes I do! If I want to keep my players, I have to go. They have to see me as key to the fun."

His hazel eyes are intent on mine. "And what about me? Do you want to keep me too?"

I look away, unable to hold his gaze. "I told you before I don't do relationships."

"That's because you were waiting for me."

I groan. "Why don't you just save us some time and have both parts of this conversation? Tell me how I feel since you seem to know so much."

"Okay. You're scared of Villroy and the family memories it holds."

I stare at him, surprised he knew that.

"You want me to be your hero, and I want that too. You care for me just as much as I care for you, and you're worried that means risking your heart. You're not sure if we're a good bet. And I'm going to save you the time figuring that out because the answer is yes. We are a good bet."

I'm speechless, my gaze shifting away. Things are good between us now, but there's still an ocean separating us. I know he'd never abandon his casino, and I can't abandon my sister or my life here. Chloe doesn't think she needs me now, but she could at any moment. I want to be close enough to go to her when she calls. I don't say any of that, though. I can only deal with one emotional thing at a time, and the big thing for me right now is what Villroy represents—the loss of the happiest times my family had. My parents—I can't catch my breath, my heart racing. Panic attack. It's been years. *No.* I will *not* fall apart. *Breathe in, breathe out.*

He brushes my hair back and then cradles my jaw, tipping my face up to his.

I meet his steady gaze and calm a little. "Ade, if I go, it has to be different. I don't want to see the cottage I rented with them. I don't want to see the north beach or anything we did before."

"I can't promise you that. It's an island. You're bound to see something that reminds you. But I can promise you that you'll be having such a good time—getting the inside tour of the casino, playing poker at some of our high-stakes tables with comps, and being with yours truly—that Villroy will become a new set of memories. The kind adult you can handle." He gives me a devilish grin. "I swear you'll love it, or your money back."

I give him a watery smile. "I'm not paying any money, you goof."

He kisses me, just a brush across my lips that leaves me wanting more. "There are other ways you can pay me."

I'm still scared of what lies ahead, but he distracts me with his kisses, hauling me into his lap and holding me close. I tell myself as long as I focus on Adrian, it'll be okay.

He stands with me in his arms, carrying me to the bedroom.

I snuggle into his warm chest. "If I have a breakdown, it's on you." I say it like I'm joking, even though I'm scared that's exactly what will happen.

"You won't have a breakdown."

"You don't know that."

"You're strong and capable. You can do this."

He sets me gently on the bed and covers me with his body. I hold on tight.

He kisses me and cradles my jaw with one hand, gazing into my eyes. "Thank you, Sara, for taking a chance on me."

My voice is shaky. "You're a good bet." I want it to be true.

He smiles, his eyes lighting up. "Now you're getting it."

He kisses me again, and I let myself go, losing myself in sensation, letting my dark thoughts fade. They'll be back soon enough.

10

Sara

Adrian and I are spending the night in the hotel suite since it's already paid for. He's asleep. It's 1 a.m. and I slip out of bed to clean up the game in the living room area. I send Chloe a quick text to let her know I'll be away for a few days in Villroy with Adrian and the guys. I don't expect her to be up, but she responds right away.

Chloe: *What time are you leaving tomorrow?*

Me: *What're you doing up so late?*

Chloe: *Reading.*

Me: *If you need me, I can cancel.*

Chloe: *I want to go with you. I'm hoping Villroy will bring back memories of Mom and Dad. I only have a few indistinct memories—Dad going off to work with his laptop bag, and Mom yelling at me to stop jumping on the sofa. I only remember that because I hit my head on the coffee table and we went to the ER. Afterward, she got me ice cream.*

Ironic how I fear triggering memories of our parents, and she yearns for them. I hadn't realized she needed that.

Chloe: *Besides, it might be hard for you to be there. I want this to be something we do together.*

I can't deny it would be easier to have her with me, and I've so missed spending time with her. She has a passport from when she travelled to Nicaragua this past summer on a service trip. I got mine at the same time so I could fly there on a moment's notice if she needed me.

Me: *What about your classes?*

Chloe: *I'll get the notes to Friday's lectures. I'm on track with studying. Don't worry.*

I smile to myself. I'm not worried about that ever.

Me: *We leave at ten a.m. I'll arrange a car to drive you to the airport.*

Chloe: *I'm excited.*

I wish I were. I'm dreading it more than anything. I text rapidly. *Good. I'm psyched to be with you. Our mini vacation.*

I'm going to pack. Goodnight.

Good night. Love you.

Love you too.

I take a deep breath. I can do this. I'll have Chloe by my side. Adrian, too, though I know he'll be busy catching up with work stuff. Plus, I'll probably be so busy with the guys I won't have time to focus on anything else. I don't have to see the two-bedroom cottage where my family crowded close every boisterous joyful summer. It's probably occupied by new summer renters. There were only ever a few cottages available to rent on the island, and the only reason we always got that one was because the elderly couple who owned it knew my father's family in France. The owners went to England every summer to visit their daughter and her family. I'll tell Chloe about the cottage in case she wants the memory jog, but I won't be going there.

I clean up, memories flooding my brain—

The scent of chocolate chip cookies fresh from the oven. Mom always baked cookies at the cottage. It was a distinctly summer activity. She was too tired after work during the school year.

My dad sitting on the small back patio with his coffee, admiring the view of the island and the sea. The cottage was near the top of the hill, the palace at the very top, and we had a spectacular view.

My father speaking French to the locals. He was from

France originally and had visited Villroy every summer as a boy. He never spoke French at home. Villroy brought out that side of him.

Long days of sun, sand, and salt water. My parents holding hands, walking everywhere. And then that summer when they stopped holding hands, and I feared they'd divorce.

I never thought they'd die. Never once crossed my mind. They were going to live forever.

A sob escapes, and I cover my mouth with my hand. I don't want Adrian to hear, so I go into the bathroom, lock the door, run the shower, and get in, letting it all out with the noise of the water and the exhaust fan covering for me. It's been so long since I cried over them. I knew this would be torture. Better than a panic attack, still, it *hurts*.

I dry off, exhausted, get dressed again, open the bathroom door, and let out a yelp.

Adrian is standing there, his gaze sympathetic.

He wraps me in his arms without a word, hugging me close. Then he guides me to bed and tucks me against his side, his arm around me. I'm getting too used to being held by him, but I don't have the strength to put up my usual defenses, keeping my distance. Instead I close my eyes and drift off to sleep.

The guys are pumped the next morning. They love the royal jet, and the moment we're on board, sitting on the tarmac, they start betting on just about everything—what time we'll arrive, the number of poker tables at the casino, and who will have the best full beard by the end of the weekend. I made arrangements with the flight crew for food, so we've got caviar on board along with champagne, vodka, and fresh fruit. Plus whatever they normally have for the meal service. I planned to put my special requests on my credit card, but Adrian insisted it was his treat.

There's four rows of reclining seats up front, as well as a

few four-chair seating areas farther back. I stay standing in the aisle, waiting for Chloe to board. The jet's still sitting on the runway.

Sergei shows up, surprising me. One of the guys must've invited him. "I hope you do not mind, Sunny Sara. I couldn't resist a comped trip." He palms my hand, giving me a folded check.

I resist the urge to peek. "Of course, you're always welcome. I'm glad to see you."

The moment he takes a seat in the back, I look at the check. It's half what he owes me. I knew he had the money! He was just agitated by having so many people witness my collection visit that day. Not to mention the fact that I turned him down. Half is a good start. Now I have the January tuition bill for Chloe and next summer's bill too. I won't be covering his bets, though, until he pays in full.

Chloe is the last to board, and the men go silent. She's in her usual cardigan, tank, and jeans. White cardigan with matching white tank today. She looks cute. When she smiles, she lights up and is truly beautiful, but she rarely smiles, only when she's excited about something she's learning or a tight smile out of politeness.

I rush over and hug her. I turn to the guys. "This is my little sister, Chloe."

Chloe lifts a hand. "Hello, Sara's friends."

I point out everyone, naming them as I go.

"Not so little, little sister Chloe," Ivan says. "All woman."

I stiffen. They'd better not even *think* about trying to get with her. But before I can say anything, Adrian crosses to her, greeting her warmly and offering to stow her backpack for her. She declines, wanting it with her to study on the flight.

I turn to Ivan. "She's only eighteen. Don't go there."

"That is old enough to marry."

"I—" Chloe starts.

I finish for her. "Chloe is here for me." I keep my voice upbeat. "And you're too old for her anyway."

"Come sit with me, little Chloe," Sergei croons from a seating area in the back.

"No, thanks," she says. "I'm sitting with Sara."

Sergei gestures to me. "Sunny Sara, join us. Let us all get to know each other better."

Adrian turns to Sergei. "Back off."

"You can't have both women," Sergei says. "Do not be selfish."

Adrian's voice is a near growl. "There's no shortage of women at the casinos on Villroy or Monte Carlo. This will all be so much more pleasant if you respect Sara's wishes. I don't want to have to kick anyone off the jet before takeoff."

Everyone shuts up.

I take a seat in the first row next to Chloe. She does her seatbelt and unzips her backpack, removing a statistics textbook.

I do my seatbelt too. "I'm not sure how much studying you'll get done with these guys around."

"Sara," she hisses, "you embarrassed me. You treat me like a child."

I'm taken aback. *Me? Embarrassing?* I'm totally chill. "These guys are too old for you."

"They look like twenties, thirties at the most."

"And you're only eighteen."

Her eyes narrow. "You do know I'm an adult, right? I've been taking care of myself for a long time."

"I took care of you."

"When you weren't working."

I suck in air. "I *had* to work. Someone had to bring in money."

The flight attendant does the safety rundown on exits and such, and we get quiet.

"I know that," she says gently once the safety speech ends. "I'm just saying that when you were working, I was on my own, and I did fine."

"You need to meet someone more like you. An academic. Sweet and gentle."

She rolls her eyes.

"What's that about? Since when do you roll your eyes at me?"

She lowers her voice. "Since you treat me like a know-nothing virgin. I can handle men fine."

My jaw gapes. She's not a virgin anymore? When did this happen? Why didn't she tell me? She tells me everything. Well, I thought she did. Then I focus on the most important thing. "Are you okay?"

"Yes. It was two summers ago."

"Two summers ago!"

She gestures to keep it down.

I lower my voice. "Why am I just hearing about it now?"

She speaks through her teeth. "Because I'm allowed to have a private life."

I flop back in my seat. I can't believe this. I'm the one who gave her the sex talk, and I was thorough too—how to protect herself, the importance of waiting for the right person, how not to get pregnant. I even gave her condoms. I told her to come to me with any questions or concerns. She never did. In fact, she seemed supremely uninterested and was so wrapped up in her studies I never even thought she had a boyfriend.

"Who was it?" I ask. "Someone from the neighborhood? From school?" Oh God. What if it was someone inappropriate like a teacher?

"Remember when I went to that three-week biomedical summer camp at Penn?"

She'd earned a scholarship to do research over the summer at the University of Pennsylvania with other gifted high school students.

"There were supposed to be chaperones," I say through my teeth. What kind of place were they running down there? Letting virgin teenaged girls run amok?

She waves a hand dismissively. "There's always ways to work around them."

I wince. "Please tell me it wasn't with a professor."

"It was Michael, another student."

Adrian takes the seat on my other side, startling me. "Nervous flyer?"

"No, I'm just...I'm okay."

The jet starts barreling down the runway, my insides

jumping right along with it. I cannot believe I'm having this conversation with Chloe two years after the fact. I thought we were so close. I tried so hard to keep the lines of communication open. What else hasn't she told me? I want to interrogate her, but I can't because Adrian is here. Anyway, I'm not sure if she'd admit anything else. Apparently, I'm no longer her confidante. I glance over once the flight smooths out, and she's gone back to studying.

"Was he nice?" I whisper.

She smiles. "He was the hottest guy there."

My jaw drops.

"Also brilliant."

"So he was your first boyfriend?"

"Not quite. More like a fellow researcher and, what did he call it? Fuck buddy."

Adrian gives my hand a squeeze and whispers in my ear, "You're much more than a fuck buddy."

I still. He overheard. I'm embarrassed on Chloe's behalf. She has fuck buddies. I mean, so do I, but I'm the adult here. Two summers ago, she was only sixteen! That's much too young. I waited until I was eighteen. Granted, that was mostly because I didn't trust any guy enough until then to even try but still. Sixteen? Gah! How did I not know? I should've noticed something different about her when she got back from camp. Big-sister fail.

Adrian kisses my cheek, temporarily halting my dark thoughts. "She's fine," he whispers. "You did your job."

My shoulders droop. I tried so hard and *still* she doesn't feel like she can come to me with important things in her life. But I can't tell Adrian any of that. Chloe is right here, and it's not the appropriate time anyway.

I nod in a jerky motion.

The pilot announces the estimated arrival time, and my stomach drops. I'm heading back to where it all began. My happy place, where the sun always shines, my parents smile and hold hands, my sister is a joyful laughing terror, and I have a best friend, who happens to be a princess, and a sweet boy friend, who is my hero.

I brace myself for the pain of a reality that can never match up.

~

Adrian

I take everyone straight to the casino the moment we arrive. It's a little after ten p.m. local time, but for us it feels more like late afternoon New York time. I'm eager to catch up on what I missed at work, and the guys are eager to play. They're all drunk. They sang Russian folk songs on the way here. I had their luggage sent ahead and their rooms prepared at the palace. I cleared it with Gabriel and Anna ahead of time, and they had our security run a background check like usual for unknown guests. No criminal records on any of them. Sara's instincts were good, and her informal network of information accurate. I'll find a quiet guest room for Chloe, away from them. I don't want her to feel harassed by their flirting. She plans to study when she's not exploring Villroy. She has no interest in the casino or spa. Sara will be with me. I need to show her exactly how she can fit both at the casino and in my life.

I set the guys up at a poker table with a comped buy-in and unlimited free drinks in a private gaming area on the second floor. Sara stays with them, determined to make herself part of the fun. I get it. She does her best to anticipate their needs and manage the experience to keep it going. If she joined me here as pit boss, she'd do the same thing on a larger scale, overseeing the customers and the staff. I'll wait to broach the topic. Step one was getting her here. My invitation to the guys was a spontaneous idea I came up with when I realized they weren't having their usual fun with their game. I went with it, knowing it would give Sara a reason to face her fear of Villroy. I did it for us. She still could've said no, and I would've known that was the end of us. I can't abandon my casino, and if she couldn't even take the risk to visit, that would've been the writing on the wall.

But she's here, and I'm all in with a long-term plan that

goes much further. If it fails, and she goes back to Brooklyn and her game, my only concern is her safely handling the money. I'll hire her a guard if it comes down to it, but I don't want it to come to that. I want her here with me for good.

I head to my office and find it locked. Strange. I knock. "Hello? Is someone in there? It's Adrian."

The door swings open to my sister Emma. Her long dark brown hair is messy like she ran her hands through it and pulled a bunch of times; her hazel eyes are huge. "Oh, thank God you're back! I literally could not take one more thing! I had to lock the door to keep any more problems from coming my way. Between the staff, the phone calls, emails, and texts, I nearly threw my phone out the window! The computer too!"

I bite back a smile, secretly pleased she thinks the job is difficult. I was beginning to think *I* was the problem. "Where's Jackson?"

"He's down at the restaurant dealing with a customer who insists on talking to the manager over what he claims is over-cooked fish. I figure the shock and awe factor over meeting Jackson should go a long way to calming him down."

"Thanks for taking over for me." She's kept in touch with me, emailing and texting about various issues. There's always something. I had no idea she was so stressed though.

She goes to the desk and grabs her purse from a drawer. "I'm so glad I'm a silent investor. That was definitely the right choice. Managing all these people is a nightmare!"

"Did they treat you strange because you were a princess?"

"They treated Jackson with kid gloves because he's a rock star. Me, they tell all their problems. And it's not just work stuff either. I'm hearing about leaking roofs and evil mothers-in-law." She flings a hand in the air. "Way too many people for me. I'm going back to my nice little music studio and my musician life."

"Huh. I wonder why they confide in you. No one has felt that comfortable with me."

"I don't know. Maybe it's because you're so reserved."

"You're reserved too." We take after our mother that way.

She smiles. "Not so much anymore. Music set me free. It

must be you. Your demeanor or something doesn't inspire oversharing." She gives my arm a squeeze. "Be glad."

"Actually, I'm kind of insulted. Were you extra sweet?"

"I don't know. I was myself. And now I'm done. You need to hire someone high level, maybe two people. This job is way too much for one person. I don't even know how you managed this long alone."

"I do have someone in mind. Sara Travers is with me."

"Sara's here? Oh wow. That's great! I haven't seen her in so long. I think she was ten last time. I was away a few summers with Mother in Italy as part of my language study. I'm going to grab Jackson and get out of here. Show me Sara on the way."

We head upstairs to the gaming room across from the restaurant. I gesture for Sara to step away from the table. She's not playing. She's background to the party.

"Emma wanted to see you again," I say when she reaches me. "Do you remember my older sister?"

Sara smiles. "Of course I remember. I've seen you at all of your many charity events, and I heard you married Jackson Walker. Congratulations."

I stare at her. She kept up with Emma? They didn't even spend much time together. Emma is two years older than us, which was a lot back then. Did she secretly keep up with me too? She did know I took honors at Cambridge, though she claimed it was something Silvia mentioned. No question in my mind now—Sara *always* wanted this connection. My chest expands with pride, a surge of affection making me want to grab her and hug her. I have to wait, but this is a fantastic sign.

"Is your sister here too?" Emma asks. "She was—" she squints for a moment "—three, I think, last time I saw her."

"Chloe," I supply.

Sara smiles proudly. "She's at the palace studying. She's a college student now."

"Ack!" Emma exclaims. "I feel so old. I'm sure she doesn't even remember me."

"She doesn't remember much from Villroy," Sara says.

"That's why she came along, hoping to jog some memories. She has little memory of our parents."

"I'm so sorry for your loss," Emma says.

Sara nods, her lips pressed tightly together. I'm sure she's heard that a lot.

"Jackson is here," Emma says. "Would you like to meet him?"

Sara brightens. "I'd love to."

The guys set their cards down and stand in a chorus of enthusiastic agreement.

Emma takes them all in. "I'll have him step in for a moment. Please continue your game. It may be a little while."

A short time later, Jackson swaggers in. He can't help it. He's a rock star.

The guys lose their shit, jumping up from the table and surrounding him. Two guards close in and gesture for some space.

"I'm a big fan!" Sergei exclaims.

"You're fantastic!"

"Your latest music is even better than the old stuff!"

"Do you still play with your band?"

Jackson is gracious, politely answering, or maybe it's just his British accent that makes him sound polite. His dirty blond hair is trimmed short, as is his beard. I introduce him to Sara, and he smiles warmly. "Nice to meet you, Sara."

She blushes pink. "If it's not too geeky, can I get your autograph?"

The guys chime in for their own autographs. A bunch of napkins are shoved in Jackson's face. He takes a seat at the poker table and asks for a pen. Emma produces one from her purse. He dutifully signs his name a bunch of times.

Finally he stands and stretches. "Right. Nice to meet you all. Emma and I need to go. Enjoy yourselves, eh?"

They head out the door, and all the guys stare after him in awe. Starstruck. I hope that was worth the trip for them. Jackson is an internationally famous rock star. Obviously they've heard of him.

I take Sara aside. "Meet me in my office when you get a chance. I want to give you the behind-the-scenes tour and show you how I'm doing the work of two people." I grin. "That's what Emma says anyway. She was so relieved to have me back."

"I'm sure," she murmurs. "Okay. I'll text you when I can get away."

I head back to the office and dig into some paperwork. Emma left the invoices to me, not wanting to muck around with money matters. That's my first step in a long list.

An hour later, my phone chimes with a text. It's Sara. She says the guys are going to the restaurant for a snack. I give her directions to find me.

When she steps inside my office a few minutes later, she looks around. "So this is where the magic happens."

"Not so much magic as a ton of work. I'm the brains, the money, and customer relations. You know what part I'm not good at?"

"Brains."

"Ha-ha. Customer relations. Staff relations too. You know me, I'd rather deal with numbers."

"You've got a real nice place here. You should be proud."

"I am, but you've hardly seen any of it."

She gestures toward the door. "I saw the lobby, the main playing area, your office, the restaurant, and the private room we have the game going in."

I stand and walk out from behind my desk. "Okay, let me introduce you to the staff, and there's still more to see. A few more rooms, the money-changing room, and a surprise upstairs."

"A sexy surprise?"

I chuckle and take her hand, entwining our fingers together. "That's for later." I guide her out of the office.

"Chloe says I kept you a secret from her."

"How's that? We all knew each other as kids."

"She says you're my boyfriend, and I never shared. She's just trying to get me to see we don't tell each other every private thing."

"Everyone has their secrets, I suppose, but we're not really a secret. You could've told her we're together."

She gets quiet, and I have the uneasy feeling that I'm all in, and she's keeping her cards close to her chest. I can't believe I'm actually the one who wants to have the relationship talk. I used to cut myself loose before the word *relationship* could even be uttered. Karma, man.

I take her to the money-changing room with its many vaults and full security staff.

"Wow!" she exclaims. "This is really fancy."

I gesture toward my assistant's office as we walk past it, empty now, and take her to the slots room.

She weaves up and down the aisles. "Noisy but fun. What's the highest pot?"

"Five hundred euro."

She lets out a low whistle. "Very nice."

I guide her out, my hand on the small of her back. "We work hard to attract high rollers. We have less expensive options too, but we want to keep the high rollers interested enough to seek us out."

"Smart."

I point out some of the guards by name and the dealers, but I don't want to interrupt them while they're working. We wrap up with the restaurant and bar, where I offer her a drink.

"Absolutely!" she says, taking a seat on a barstool. I'm glad she's enjoying herself so far.

"Sara! Join us!" The guys are all waving her over from a table with plenty of lobsters and a pile of crab legs.

"After my drink I will," she calls with a sunny smile. Sunny Sara. No, she's *my* Sara.

"How late do you stay open?" she asks.

"We're open eleven a.m. to two a.m. Staff works in shifts. I'm usually here the whole time."

"So this is like your whole life." She gestures in a wide circle. "You work, sleep, work."

"Basically. But I'm sure it's like that for most new businesses."

Her drink arrives, a martini, along with my beer. She sucks on the olive and my trousers get tight.

I take a sip of beer, trying to cool down.

"That's not how my job goes," she says, sipping her martini. "I've got lots of free time. It's awesome."

"And what do you do with your free time?"

"I'm networking, always looking for new players, especially fish with deep pockets. And I'm scouting out restaurants for new menu ideas and interesting locations. I try to keep it fresh."

"So your free time is actually your work time?"

"I work out too. Daily run."

"When do you have free time for your friends?"

Her eyes shift to the side. "I work it in here and there." I suspected she kept to herself. Chloe is the only real connection she has, and Chloe is all grown up.

"You should work here," I say.

She smiles nervously and sips her martini.

I lean close. "I could really use your help."

She shakes her head.

"Why not?"

"Adrian! Again with the why not."

"It's a valid question."

"Because I have a life back home. I have Chloe. And I'm not sure I could ever be comfortable here."

"You will be. You feel comfortable so far, right?"

"Yes, but we came in at night. All I saw was the yacht, the car, and the casino."

"Tonight you'll see the palace."

"In the dark. Plus I've never seen your room before, so I know it won't trigger anything for me."

"That's good. It'll be a new memory for you. I want to build new Villroy memories with you."

She drains her martini. "Tomorrow's going to be hard seeing it all in the daylight."

"I'll be with you every step of the way. In the meantime, think about being my right-hand woman. We can run the place together. Me more in the background working the financials and marketing strategy, you managing staff and customer relations. I'll pay you a fantastic salary. You can live at the palace with me, or we can find you a place nearby if you're not ready to live with me yet. I can be very patient as long as you're in my life."

She slowly blinks and then shakes her head like she can't quite believe my offer. "Do you still think what I'm doing back home is all that dangerous?"

"The way you handle the money is dangerous, the way you operate alone, the personal financial risk you take to cover bets. With so much money it can attract the wrong sort of person. What if something happened to you? Then who will be there for Chloe?"

Her eyes tear up, and she blinks rapidly. "I never thought of it that way. I did this for her. It was all a calculated risk."

My eye catches on the guys' movements, and I jerk my chin toward them. "Your players seem harmless."

We both watch as two of the guys battle each other with crab legs. We laugh.

I get serious again. "You'd be perfect for this job."

She looks wary.

"It's not a proposal. I'm just asking you to consider the job." I tuck her hair behind her ear, stroking her cheek with my thumb. "And I want you to be with me, if that part wasn't clear."

Her green eyes search my face, like she's looking for some measure of my sincerity. I am sincere, and I'm in love with her. I know she's not ready to hear that yet. One step at a time. I can't lose her after waiting so many years to find her again.

11

Sara

The next afternoon, we're all back at the casino, except for Chloe, who stayed in her room to study. I briefly saw the day spa this morning, but I'm not comfortable with the intimacy of a massage, so there wasn't much of a draw for me there. All of the guys had massages, some of them even had facials. I was shocked. While they did that, I shadowed Adrian as he worked, checking on different issues that cropped up. I have to admit it's interesting work. It's like what I do, but in one interconnected world. I could see getting comfortable in this environment; it's like its own little neighborhood. The staff work in a united purpose—entertainment. That's the business I'm in.

The guys are jetting over to Monte Carlo for dinner tonight and more gambling. I plan on going with them, even though Adrian wants me to stay here with him. He doesn't understand that I need to always be connected in my players' minds to the game. *I* bring the fun. *I* make the arrangements. I'm Sunny Sara in the background they can always turn to with any request. Well, almost any request.

We're all on the rooftop terrace for poker with a view when Adrian appears. He crosses to our table, leans down, and kisses my cheek. I flush with heat at his casual affection, and I suddenly realize I'm smiling. He got under my skin with his casual confidence that we belonged together. I'm starting to believe him. My Adrian, my hero.

He turns to the guys. "Anyone here a Yankees fan?"

A retired Yankees player appears on the terrace, and my guys are on their feet. They practically stampede over to him, and then a few more baseball players appear. All of them retired, some Yankees, some from other teams. Nothing like professional athletes to bring out the little boy in full-grown men.

Next thing I know, we've got two tables going with the ball players and my guys intermingled. My guys rotate after a round so everyone can get a chance to meet every player. I make sure I get to know everyone and let them know I organize awesome games in Brooklyn. My guys are having a blast, which makes me happy.

By the time Adrian announces the jet's ready to take them to Monte Carlo, everyone is buddy buddy.

Ivan pulls me aside. "Thank you so much for this trip. These guys are incredible."

I beam my Sunny Sara smile. "My pleasure. Adrian was also a help. Pays to have great connections."

"It does. Listen, Mario invited us to his game in Manhattan next week. It's all former Yankees players and some Mets. A few current guys too. They rotate in, depending on who's in town. They said they have room for us. They play a room with several tables. You understand, yes? It's too good an opportunity to pass up."

My stomach drops. "Sure, have fun. Just one game, right?"

His eyes are back on his new friends. "Depends. We'll see." He meets my eyes. "I just want to be straight with you."

Shit. I'm losing them. Pro athlete poker. Bigger pot, more fan-boy excitement. I can't compete with that, and I know it. I want to cry. The game is falling apart right in front of my eyes. The best, most lucrative job I've ever had.

"Still on for the following week, right?" I ask, trying not to sound desperate.

"I'll let you know," he mutters before rejoining the group.

I've lost my game. I can't believe this. One chance meeting with a ball player and it's all over? We've been doing great for more than two months. I finally felt like I could breathe, my money problems solved. Now I'm going to have to start all over again. Manhattan is run by Lee Tran. I would be black-balled or worse for trying to poach. I'll have to try again in Brooklyn fast before someone else sets up a more desirable game. Or shift farther out to Long Island, which is basically like starting with a blank slate, trying to make connections and find the best venues. Su-u-uck!

Adrian appears by my side. "You still want to go with them to Monte Carlo? They seem pretty content with their new friends."

The guys are all talking, laughing, slapping each other on the back.

I feel peevish in light of their obvious happiness. "Did you *have* to bring the ball players up here?"

"It's the first time those players were here. I was excited to see them too. Jackson is the one who had the connection and invited them. He just didn't know when they would show."

I sigh as the guys file out with their new friends, so busy yukking it up they don't even notice I'm not with them. My eyes sting. "I've lost them," I say quietly. "There's no point in tagging along."

Adrian drops an arm over my shoulders. "I'm sure you didn't lose them forever. They just want to have some fun tonight. And the best part is I get you all to myself."

I shrug his arm off. "Ivan told me they're moving to a new game in Manhattan with the ball players next week. They'll stay there as long as they can—bigger pot, celebrity athletes. I can't compete with that, and I can't horn in on the game either. Someone else runs Manhattan."

"Did you run Brooklyn?"

"I was getting there. That was the next step. There's a few other private poker games, but mine was the best." I look up to the sky, trying to keep the tears from escaping.

"Sara, it wasn't my intention to ruin your game. I was trying to add to the fun with the ball players."

I blink rapidly and dash at a tear with my fist. "They're having fun all right."

He gives my shoulder a squeeze. "You want to shadow me again? Saturday night is our busiest night."

"Actually, I think I'll head back to the palace and spend time with Chloe." I take a deep breath. "If I can tear her away from her studies. The girl is nonstop."

"Okay. Good luck with that. I'll call for a car to take you up to the palace, and catch up with you tonight."

I nod woodenly.

"Are you okay?"

"No, but I will be." That's me, always hustling to make sure everything is heading in the right direction.

"You can wait in my office until the car gets here."

"I'll wait out front." I try for a smile but can't manage it.

I manage to keep it together all the way out of the casino before bursting into tears.

Ugh. I wipe my tears away furiously. They accomplish nothing. I have to keep my head clear and think of next steps. I walk around the building to take in the view of the sea. It's near sunset, beautiful, but I can't appreciate it. And because I already feel shitty, I recklessly look over to the north beach, where most of my memories are, but the view is blocked by the spa. I remember there was a black rock. It always seemed so far off in the distance. Adrian dared me to race to it. Of course I did. I remember treading water and telling him about my parents fighting and my fear that they'd divorce, and then when we started to race back, I sliced my foot open, probably on a submerged rock.

The memory isn't too difficult for me. Adrian stayed with me until I met up with my mom at the health clinic. I got a lot of special attention at home, everyone fussing over me, even five-year-old Chloe brought me snacks so I wouldn't have to hobble around on my hurt foot. Maybe I *could* see the north beach again. I bet it's exactly the same. Adrian said the only part of the island that was developed since the last time I was here was the spa and casino.

I'll wait to see it with Chloe. It's only around five o'clock. We should have time.

The car Adrian requested for me pulls into the lot a short while later and gives me a ride up the long winding road to the palace. We're going to pass my old cottage. It's the first time I'll see it in daylight. This morning when I drove down with Adrian, I purposely focused on him instead of looking at it, pretending I was unaware of it. Now that I've already cried, I don't feel like I'm hanging on so tightly to my control. Like it wouldn't be such a sudden rush of emotions that would overwhelm, but more like another wave of water. My foundation is already rocked. I know I have to start over again. I don't think I could feel any worse, and maybe it would make me feel better. A healing of sorts.

Oh! There it is! It's exactly like I remember—white with a blue door, blue window boxes, and blue shutters. It's a two-bedroom single-story cottage. There's a patio out back with a view. I wonder if the elderly couple still lives there. Suddenly I want to see the inside, but I'll wait to get Chloe first.

Adrian was right. Adult me can handle this. I definitely would've had a breakdown seeing all this when I was still a struggling teen trying to keep our little family together, but now it's doable. In fact, I feel stronger already. My parents loved this place, and they wanted my sister and me to have carefree summers out in nature with fresh air and the sea, away from the stifling hot summer in the city. I'm lucky I had Villroy in my life. That was a gift they gave me, and it gave me Adrian and Silvia too. I feared Villroy and its memories for so long, but it was always just a gift.

A sense of peace washes over me. I really want to share this with my sister.

I go back to the palace and head straight for Chloe's room. She's not there. I text her. *Where are you?*

No reply.

My heart is in my throat. *Okay, do not panic.* She often turns off her phone when she's studying. I find a servant and ask if they know where she is, but they don't. Then I ask for directions to the palace library, but she's not there either. I try the gardens. No dice. I text her again and tell her to get back to me so we can tour Villroy together. I'm ready now.

I wander through the gardens, which I've never been to before, and find myself down at the beach. I sit there for a while, thinking hard. I'll go through my waiting list of players and start a new game. The problem is most of my waiting list are friends of my guys, who will probably hear about the other Manhattan game and want to get in on that. I could go back to waitressing, look for an office manager position, too, but that was such an exhausting grind. Then there's Adrian. He offered me a job here, a place to live free of charge. It's ideal in many ways, but it's also a commitment to him. What if it doesn't work out? Then I'm stuck here and he's my boss. That could get ugly.

And then there's Chloe. I can't live so far from her. I know she still needs me, even if she thinks she doesn't.

I check my phone. No response from her. I stand up and brush the sand off me. Where could she be? It's an island, so she couldn't have gone far. I'm too wound up to sit any longer, so I decide to do the tour of summers past by myself. Maybe it's better this way. If I break down in tears, no one has to witness it. I've always tried to be strong for Chloe.

As soon as I get back inside the palace, I ask the first servant I see for a driver to take me around. It's not long before a Mercedes pulls up to the courtyard, and I hop in the front seat. I smile at the driver, a thin man in his fifties wearing a cap over his bald head. "Hi, thank you for driving me. I'm Sara."

"Yes, ma'am. We all know who you are. I'm Antoine."

Really? They all know who I am? Maybe Adrian had to clear my stay and inform everyone. "Nice to meet you, Antoine. I'd like to see the north beach."

He inclines his head and then we're off. We pass my old cottage on the way down. There's a light on in there. I imagine the elderly couple shuffling around, maybe getting dinner ready.

As soon as the beach comes into view, I see the black rock. It's just as big and imposing as I remember. Wow. We really swam out far, considering we were only twelve. It's way past the breakers.

"I'll just be a few minutes," I tell Antoine.

"Take your time, ma'am."

"Thanks."

I step out of the car and make the long walk down to the beach. I stop to take off my shoes and socks and let my toes dig into the soft sand, closing my eyes for a moment as memories flood my mind—sandcastles, digging for crabs, smoothing spots out for the perfect picnic blanket placement, the cabana and our sand card-playing area. I open my eyes and breathe deep. It's all good. I'm okay.

I spent most of my time here with Adrian, Silvia, and Chloe, plus an entourage of guards and a nanny. My parents joined us sometimes, but I think they also liked having their couple time. I never asked them what they did when we were here. Maybe they went to another beach and set out a couple of chaise lounges, enjoying the peace and quiet away from the city and their two rowdy daughters. Chloe was the truly rowdy one. I was just exuberant and enthusiastic. I want to be that girl again instead of feeling so bogged down by heavy responsibility.

I keep walking toward the sea, letting the waves run over my feet. The water is cooler than it was in the summer now that it's early October, but not too much. I bend and run my fingers through the baby waves too. I turn. The beach is empty, but I can picture my last summer here so vividly—me and Adrian playing poker in the cabana. Chloe and Silvia building an elaborate sandcastle. Bike riding. Swimming. Silvia reading.

Adrian and Silvia grew into the fully bloomed versions of their kid selves. Silvia went from bookworm to book editor, and Adrian went from an ace poker player to a card shark running his own casino. It's just me and Chloe who don't match up. The break in our path to adulthood was too harsh to let us bloom on that same path. Chloe should've been a free spirit, maybe marching for Greenpeace or something, instead of a serious no-fun student. And me? I feel like I'm just starting to get back to what I truly enjoy—poker—after slogging through a never-ending struggle.

The breeze feels like a caress over my skin, ruffling my hair. This wasn't so bad. In fact, I feel really good about seeing my life with a new clarity. I head back to the driver and direct him to the cottage. I'm hoping the couple who lives there won't mind letting me take a peek inside. I only met them a couple of times as they were on their way out, but I'll just remind them who I am. They should be friendly enough. They knew my dad's family in France.

It's not a far drive, and I'm surprisingly calm as I walk up to the front door and ring the bell. The light's still on in the living room, and there's an old Renault parked in the driveway.

I press the bell again. This time I hear heavy footsteps. The door springs open to a young shirtless guy with impressive muscles, wearing jeans and nothing else. His blond hair is short, his angular features a little intimidating. A tough guy. What happened to the elderly couple?

I plow ahead. "Hello, I'm Sara Travers. My family used to rent this cottage when I was a kid, and I was hoping to take a peek inside for old times' sake."

"Sara?" a familiar feminine voice calls.

"Chloe!"

12

———

Sara

I cannot believe my eyes. Chloe is naked with a light blue bedsheet wrapped around her. My eyes snap back to tough guy. A murderous rage pumps through my blood. "What the hell is going on here? How old are you?"

He looks back to Chloe. "I'll leave you to your visitor." He swaggers back to the bedroom. I hope to get dressed.

Seriously, WTF. I step inside. "What is happening right now?" I know, but I don't want it to be true. She's eighteen! She does not know this man!

Chloe sighs. "Relax. It's no big deal."

I scowl and cross my arms. "I thought you were studying."

"I was, but then I thought, how often will I be in Villroy? I should see more of it."

"Yes, Villroy! Not—" I jab a finger in the direction of the bedroom "—whoever that is! We were supposed to see the cottage together."

The sheets slips, and she readjusts it around her. *I can't even.* "I know, but you were busy with your game, and I didn't want to wait."

I stare as the man who defiled my sister steps out of the

bedroom, wearing a snug gray T-shirt with his jeans, and casually walks into the kitchen.

"Who is that guy?" I whisper fiercely.

"Michael. He's a palace guard."

"Do you only sleep with guys named Michael?" That was the name of her fuck buddy from nerd camp.

She smiles, her head tilting to the side. "How funny. I hadn't made the connection. Totally random."

"So you just showed up here, asked for the tour, and stripped naked?"

"More like I asked for the tour, he was kind enough to give it to me, and I only remembered the kitchen. We sat and had some tea."

"And then he ripped your clothes off?" I'm sure Michael was the aggressor here. The man oozes testosterone. I'll kick his ass, or at least go to his boss. Adrian will definitely hear about this. Palace guards are supposed to protect, not seduce innocent student visitors.

"Is that how your dates go?" Chloe asks with an amused look.

"This isn't funny! And it's not about me. What am I supposed to think? You're wearing a bedsheet."

"I'm not sure why I have to explain myself to you, but here it is, the whole sordid story. Ready?"

I nod once, trying to keep a neutral expression while bracing myself for the worst. The lines of communication are open.

She goes on. "I explained why I was here to Michael, you know, trying to remember our parents. He shared that he's also an orphan. We talked for a while, and then he invited me to stay for dinner. I suggested a kiss instead, and he took the hint. Things progressed nicely from there."

Some hint. I run a hand through my hair. No judgment. She shared—lines of communication are good—and that's the important part. "Okay, so get dressed. Then you can give me the tour, and we'll go back to the palace for dinner."

She looks toward the kitchen, where Michael is. "I want to

stay here a little longer. He says he'll take me back to the palace whenever I want. I'll text you when I'm on my way."

"I texted you earlier, you know."

She smiles, her green eyes sparkling. "I was busy at the time."

I clench my jaw. My little sister has fuck buddies. I didn't want this for her. I wanted her to have boyfriends, guys who treat her special. I wanted her to have everything I couldn't have. I'm the broken one. I dedicated myself to keeping her whole.

"Sara, you said you wanted me to have some fun in college, so now I am."

"This isn't college!" I work for a level, reasonable tone. "And I didn't mean this kind of fun."

She shrugs and her sheet slips, exposing her boob. There's a bite mark. I jerk my gaze away.

"Oops," she says. "Be back in a few."

I stand there, arms crossed, silently seething. Who is this woman?

And that's when it hits me. Chloe is a full-grown woman. She has to make her own decisions now, her own mistakes. I have to stop mothering her.

"Would you like some tea, Sara?" Michael asks, leaning casually in the archway that separates the kitchen from the living room.

"No, thank you," I say through my teeth.

He straightens. "In answer to your earlier question, I'm twenty-six. I was given this cottage to live in by the royal family because I'm captain of the guards. I run their training regimen."

The royal family owns this cottage now? Was it done out of respect for my parents? Did the elderly couple die or move away? It's strange that the royal family would buy this particular cottage.

"Do they own other cottages and let staff use them?" I ask.

"This is the only one that I know of."

So strange. I should ask Adrian.

Chloe returns dressed in a tank top and jeans with her

usual white Keds. "Ready for the tour?" she asks brightly. Someone's in a good mood after getting laid. *Don't think about it.*

"Sure," I mumble, still reeling from the shock of my sister hooking up with some rando. I take a deep breath. I need to let her live her life on her terms.

She crosses to me, her eyes sympathetic. "Sorry. I don't have the memories you do. I don't mean to make light of it. Are you really okay looking around? I could just share what I remember later, or not. Whatever works for you."

My eyes tear up because she's a truly caring person, and I know I had something to do with that. I give her arm a squeeze. "Thanks, but I think I'll be okay. I came here because after I went to the north beach, I realized Mom and Dad wanted us to have these wonderful summers here away from the city. Villroy was a gift they gave us."

She nods once. "We were lucky to come here. It's beautiful, and how lucky were we to be friends with a prince and a princess? I didn't understand who they were when I was little. I thought they were just local kids with lots of babysitters."

I smile. "Yeah, their guards and nanny were always with us. Adrian and Silvia were a gift to us too. They were really nice to both of us, and you were not easy when you were little. You were a devilish whirlwind, always up to something."

Her eyes light up. "Like what?"

"Skinny-dipping in the ocean and running all over the beach naked."

She laughs. "I have no memory of that."

"Pretending you were Godzilla and destroying the sand-castles that Silvia helped you make, throwing our lunch to the seabirds, pulling the legs off crabs. Oh my God, one time you put a tiny fish in your mouth and accidentally swallowed it!"

She crinkles her nose. "*Eww.* Why would I do that?"

I giggle. "You thought you could keep it alive in the spit in your mouth and take it home as a pet. You were really upset when we told you it was gone forever."

She smiles. "I'm glad you're okay to talk about this stuff now. It worried me that you shut yourself off from what I remembered as a blur of sunny happy days."

I let out a breath. "I remember them that way too. I think reconnecting with Adrian and Silvia made it easier to get back to this place. I cried over Mom and Dad when I first decided to come here, and I think that actually helped. I feel at peace."

She hugs me. "I'm so glad." She pulls away and gestures to the room. "You've seen the living room, and this over here is the kitchen."

Michael appears again in the kitchen archway and purposely doesn't move out of the way as Chloe tries to get by. She smiles up at him, her hands on his massive biceps as she slides across his front to pass. He grins down at her and then steps out of the kitchen, gesturing for me to pass.

I join Chloe in the small kitchen. "Oh! I remember this! It's exactly the same." The white and black checkered floor, the glossy wood table and chairs with cushions on them. I turn. The sink and faucet are the same. "They updated the appliances and took down the seashell wallpaper and white lace curtains."

I stand in front of the sink and look out the window. There's a view of the next cottage, mostly, but if I crane my neck a bit, there's a view of the sea.

I turn back to Chloe. "What do you remember about the kitchen?"

"Strangely, I remembered the floor. I mostly remember playing on the beach."

I follow her out and down the hall toward the bedrooms. I poke my head into the bathroom on the way. They've updated it with a new sink, countertop, and tile. Everything white. "I think this used to be beige," I say.

I take one look in the open door of the bedroom that used to be my parents' and turn away, not because it reminds me of them. Because it has a king-sized bed with rumpled light blue sheets. The same light blue sheet that was recently wrapped around my sister.

She pushes open the door to where she and I used to sleep. The old furniture is gone, the old rug, and it's been painted from its cheery yellow to an off white. Now it's a music room with a keyboard, acoustic guitar, fiddle, and a small bookcase with sheet music. On top of the bookcase is a harmonica.

"Your guard is a musician," I say, surprised. I thought he'd be hurling telephone poles for fun. Something barbaric like that.

Chloe nods. "He's multifaceted. He said he'd play something for me after dinner. Would you like to stay for dinner?"

"That's okay. I'll leave you to your date."

She snorts. "This isn't a date. It's just a one-night stand."

I press my lips together. "Did he tell you that?"

"No, I told him that. I'm leaving tomorrow, and he belongs here. It works out perfectly for everyone."

"Will you stay in touch?"

She lifts one shoulder. "I don't see the point."

Have I failed her in this too? My lack of ties to other people has set a bad example, and now she's afraid to connect in a meaningful way. I don't want her to be like me. I want her to have everything I didn't have—college, parties, friends, relationships.

I put my hand on her arm. "It might seem scary, but some-times it's worth taking a chance on someone. You know, letting them into your heart."

She gives me a soft smile. "Are you trying to tell me you want to stay here with Adrian?"

I drop my hand from her arm, my heart working double time. "I was talking about you."

"I'm fine. I told you I'm working toward something. Harvard Medical School is my dream, and you taught me to work hard for my dreams."

"Not to the exclusion of having a life."

"This is my life. There's nothing else I want or need right now. I'll look for a relationship when I have the time and energy to devote to one. Okay? You can relax about me. Now it's my turn to look out for you. If you have feelings for

Adrian, which I think you do, you have my blessing to stay here on Villroy and see where it goes. I'll visit you on school breaks." She smiles. "It's not such a hardship for me to visit you at a palace on a beautiful island. It's time *you* let someone into *your* heart."

I stare at her, unable to speak over the lump in my throat. Everything I wanted for her she wants for me too. And maybe it's time I let myself have that.

She gives my arm a reassuring squeeze. "I want you to be happy."

Gah! I wipe my eyes, laughing at the same time as a lightness comes over me. "Are you sure? You're really okay?"

"I'm more than okay. I'm happy with my life just as it is."

I sniffle. "Adrian did offer me a job here."

"Then take it."

I hug her and more tears leak out of my eyes. When I pull back, she's still dry-eyed. She really is fine with it. "I love you, Chloe."

She beams, her face lighting up. "I love you too."

We head back to the living room.

"Bye, Michael," I call. "Thank you for letting us see the cottage."

"No problem at all," he says with a hint of amusement. Ah, yes, it worked out for him nicely. La-la-la, not thinking about it.

Chloe walks me to the door.

I glance at Michael waiting behind her to resume their amorous night, and look back to her, my poker face firmly in place. "So I'll see you tonight? Or tomorrow for the flight home?"

She smiles. "Probably tomorrow." She leans close to whisper, "He's *much* better than the first Michael. I'll catch a ride back to the palace with him when he goes to work in the morning."

I paste on a smile. "Great. See you then."

I head back to my waiting car. There's only one person I want to be with right now. I'm ready for what he's offering, ready to take a leap of faith. I'm betting on us.

13

———

When I texted Adrian to meet up, he asked me to meet him in the casino restaurant for dinner. He's already at a table for two when I get there, and waves me over with a warm smile.

A surge of affection rushes through me. My prince, my hero, my *love*. I do love him. Maybe I always have.

My heart pounds, a lightness to my limbs as I cross the room. I'm about to expose my most vulnerable self, take a giant leap of faith, and commit to living here with him. It's the most terrifying thing I've ever done in my life, but I'm ready. Only with Adrian would this be possible. Our connection spanned the miles and years and still remained so strong. We were always meant to be.

He gets out of his seat to give me a kiss before guiding me over to a chair and pulling it out for me. I let myself enjoy his special treatment. My Adrian is a prince not just by blood but by his actions. I'm so lucky I met him when we were just kids. In a way, I can thank my parents for giving me this connection. He's part of me just like I'm part of him.

He smiles at me across the table, his eyes warm on mine. "You're looking a lot happier than earlier."

"I am. I was feeling so shitty I figured the hell with it, I may as well take the tour down memory lane, and it really wasn't what I feared it would be. I mostly remembered being with you and Silvia on the beach, and my memories of the cottage are forever changed by finding Chloe naked with a strange man there." I hold up a palm before he can go he-man protective. "No worries. It was totally consensual."

He barks out a laugh. "Michael lives there now, the guard captain. Great guy, I know him well. So him and Chloe?"

"Yes. And I do *not* want to talk about that."

"Understood."

"Did you know your family owns the cottage now?"

"Yes. Silvia and I grieved the loss of your family here. We asked our parents to buy the cottage after we got back from the funeral so you and Chloe could come back to visit even if you didn't have the money to rent it for the summer. My parents made the couple who lived there an offer, and they were happy to take it so they could move closer to their daughter." He leans across the table and takes my hand in his. "Silvia said she asked you to come several times. She told you it was free."

My jaw goes slack. "I didn't know she meant it that way. I thought she was offering to pay for us and that's why it was free."

He gives my hand a squeeze. "We missed you."

My eyes well. I have not been near tears so many times in years. Villroy, no, *Adrian* opened up something inside me I thought was closed forever—my heart. It's all so new and raw but worth it. So worth it. I can finally let love in.

"I wasn't ready then," I manage over the tightness in my throat. "But thank you to you and your wonderful family."

"Well, as you can see, we let Michael stay there after it seemed like you weren't coming back. You could always stay with me when you're here."

I smile. "I'd like that." I take a deep breath, about to declare I'm ready to stay, but the words get stuck in my throat. I'm a mess of raw emotions and it's so hard to express them.

The waitress arrives to take our order, and the moment passes.

Over dinner, Adrian is unusually talkative, filling me in on all the ins and outs of the casino. I get the feeling he's bringing me up to speed in hopes that I'll take his job offer. He really wants what I could bring to his casino. I like that he values my potential contribution to the casino that obviously means so much to him.

By the time we finish dinner, I'm ready to make my move. "Let's go back to your office."

He raises his brows. "Business or pleasure?"

"Business," I say on a laugh.

We make the short walk to his office, and I take the chair across from his desk. "Okay, let's make it official. I'll sign an employment contract and be your pit boss and right-hand woman."

"Great," he says brusquely, taking his seat behind the desk. "Let me just print out the paperwork, and we'll be on our way."

That's it? I thought he'd be happier that I'm willing to live and work on Villroy. With him. Did he miss the part that I'm here not just to help at the casino but to be with him?

Apparently, yes. He just stepped out of the room to the printer in his assistant's office.

I think I didn't do this right. I need to really open up, admit I'm so in love with him I'm willing to commit to a real long-term relationship, even though it scares the hell out of me that he'll leave. Or more likely I'll have to be the one to leave since we're on his island home. Should I just blurt it out? *I love you,* or maybe, *Adrian, we had a pact.* My knee bounces. Is that too forward? Will he think I'm proposing? For the second time? Ugh!

I'm about to drop my head on the desk in complete despair over my inexperience with relationships and all the heavy emotional talk that goes with them, when he returns.

He hands me the papers, instructing me to read them over, sign when I'm ready, and reminding me to bring my official ID for their records. It's all very professional.

I'm moving thousands of miles away to be with the man I've finally decided to let into my heart, and he's acting like Mr. Professional Boss.

I lift my gaze from the papers. He's back behind his desk, staring at his computer. "Is this going to be awkward to have you as my boss? People will know I'm sleeping with the boss."

One corner of his mouth lifts in a small smile. "You and I will be at an equal level, co-managers; therefore, I won't technically be your boss. And I'm more than capable of being a professional at work."

I'm irritated but rise to the challenge. "So am I."

"Great."

"It is great."

"After you sign the papers, we'll get right to work."

And we actually do.

I'm so confused. I thought this meant something more than work. My heart is outside my chest—exposed and vulnerable—and it's too late to lock it up tight. It's reaching for him.

By the time we drive back to the palace, I've given up my silly romantic fantasy of Adrian being overcome with joy. He needed me as co-manager, he wants me in his bed, and I have way overplayed my hand. Lowering expectations now.

When we get to his suite, he turns to me. "Have a seat. I have something I want to show you." He gestures to a cushy leather reclining chair in the living room.

"Happy to. I love this chair." I sit down and recline it all the way back, so it's practically like a bed.

"I'll get you a matching one," he says as he pulls a framed Escher print off the wall.

I jackknife back to a sitting position. "Now that's a great hiding place for a safe."

"Shh, don't tell," he says while he does the combination.

"Is that your stash of cash?" I ask.

"It's all of my valuables." He pockets something and palms something.

I'm on the edge of my seat. What secret is he about to reveal?

He crosses to my chair and produces two cards with a flourish from the palm of his hand. I let out a breath. It's the pair of fives from his dragon card set—a heart and a diamond.

"You really did keep them," I whisper.

His eyes are direct. "We had a pact."

"Did you always believe we'd reunite at twenty-five?"

"I hoped."

I leap up and throw my arms around his neck, hugging him tight. "I did too. I always secretly hoped, but I was too chicken to admit it."

He tips my chin up. "One thing you have never been is chicken."

My eyes sting. "I was. I avoided you and Silvia and Villroy, scared that it would be too difficult to face the memories. If you hadn't shown up on my doorstep—"

"It was inevitable. I'm your hero. The hero always swoops in when called upon."

"But I didn't call you."

"When we both turned twenty-five, that's what we said, and we're still twenty-five." He hands me the cards. "These are yours."

I clutch them tightly, staring at them. "Mine are still in the safe at home." I lift my gaze to his. "I kept them in a fireproof safe, just like my heart, locked up tight, and you burned right through it. Only you could've gotten through."

He smiles. "And you had it in an oven too."

We laugh.

"I wish I had my cards here to put them together." I set his pair on the end table.

"That's okay. We'll get them when we get your stuff."

"So we're really doing this? Living and working together?"

He kisses me. "Among other things, I hope. Do you remember what else we said the day of our pact?"

I nod once. "Matching pairs, hearts and diamonds, twos and fives just like at a wedding. Two hearts, two diamonds. And you said guys don't wear diamonds."

He goes down on one knee. "That's right, love. I said I'd give you two diamonds." He holds up a diamond engagement ring with two large round diamonds set at an angle from each other, surrounded by smaller diamonds, on a platinum band.

"I think I'm hyperventilating."

He grins. "You can't be hyperventilating if you're still speaking."

"When did you get this?"

"When I was in New York. I knew it was inevitable, and I knew exactly what I wanted for you."

My knees go weak, and I slowly sit down again.

"Sara Travers, will you honor the pact we made so long ago and be my wife?"

"Yes!" Tears stream down my face, happy tears, as he slides the ring on my finger.

He rises to his feet and pulls me into his arms. "I love you. I always have and I always will."

"I love you too. I so regret not getting in touch sooner. We wasted so much time."

"No regrets. You and I happened exactly when we were meant to. You had to finish raising Chloe, and now she's off on her own, doing fantastic."

"You're right. Chloe needed me, but I should've kept in touch." I squeeze him tight.

He strokes my hair. "No more looking back. We're here together now." He lifts my hand, showing off my engagement ring. "And I've got you forever."

I kiss him. "Yes! Happily so. I hope you don't mind if Chloe stays here on her school breaks."

He holds my jaw, his thumb stroking the sensitive spot just under my ear. "Of course not. She's family. I expected her to stay with us. She's welcome anytime for as long as she likes. I'll cover her tuition. I don't want you to worry about that."

I'm so touched by his inclusion of my sister I can't speak for a moment. Finally, I manage to say in a hoarse voice, "Thank you so much for understanding about her, but you don't have to cover her tuition. She's my responsibility."

"She's family," he repeats. "I take care of my family, and I'm going to make you partner in the casino with me. It's you, me, Emma, and Jackson, each with a say on the running of the casino, each receiving a portion of the profits."

My jaw drops. "Did you buy out a portion of their share to include me?" That must've cost a lot.

"I would have, but they said it wasn't necessary. They understand now how much work it is for us, and I've told them how much you bring to the table. They're happy to remain in the background, occasionally performing, but otherwise silent investors."

I blink. "It's too much."

His voice is warm honey, and I melt, my knees going weak. "It's my wedding gift to you, love."

I cannot believe this. Me, part owner of a casino? It's beyond my wildest dreams. Of course it is, because it's from Adrian Rourke, the man who surpasses all my wildest dreams.

"Do you accept?" he asks.

"Yes! Of course I accept! Thank you!" I hug him tight and then pull back to look up at him. "I'll pay Chloe's tuition from my casino earnings. This is just beyond…Adrian." My voice cracks. "I want to give you an amazing wedding gift too. I'll have to think of something really great."

"You already did by agreeing to marry me and live here with me. It's everything I've always wanted."

"There must be something. What do you want in your wildest dreams?"

He strokes my hair back, his eyes intent on mine. "Cards on the table?"

"Absolutely."

"I want a family with you, when you're ready."

I nod, my vision swimming with tears. "I want that too, but that's a gift for both of us. What else do you want?"

He gives me a sexy smile and inclines his head toward the bedroom. "I have some ideas."

"Anything."

He growls in my ear in the deep voice that gives me hot shivers, "Not only are you a dream come true, you're about to make every fantasy come true."

EPILOGUE

Three months later...

Adrian

It's official! Sara and I are married. We're on our way to the ballroom for our wedding reception after taking a million pictures right after the ceremony. It's a few days after Christmas. We didn't want to wait long to marry after waiting so many years to connect again. We also wanted it at a time when we knew a lot of our family would have some time off to return to Villroy for the holidays.

She's been a huge help to me at the casino right from the start, just as I knew she'd be. After a couple of months, we hired someone to open and do some routine checks before she and I work the late shift together, me mostly in my office, Sara mostly on the floor. We switch it up sometimes, but that's how it works best. We're both night owls. She's better at managing people, and I'm better at numbers and big-picture strategy. It was probably the easiest and best decision I ever made. I mean, besides marrying her.

As we approach the ballroom, I'm anticipating a huge cheer and applause like at the palace chapel right after we said "I do" followed by a lot of social time. I need her just to myself for a moment longer. I pull her around the corner to a quiet hallway.

"Where are we going?" she asks.

"Here," I say before wrapping my arms around her and pressing my lips to hers.

She throws her arms around my neck and kisses me passionately. The fire ignites between us, and I'm suddenly dying for more. I pin her against the wall, pressing my body against hers. *Yesss.* I kiss a trail to her jaw, up to her ear, where I growl in the way that makes her hot and needy, "Upstairs."

She gazes into my eyes. "I have a wedding gift for you."

"You already framed the cards from our pact, and you honored our pact. That's the best gift you could give me." The framed cards are hanging on the wall just above our bed as a constant reminder that our love was meant to be. Our younger selves knew.

I kiss her again, demanding more. She melts against me in the way I love.

Several moments later, she tears her mouth away, breathing hard. "Ade, listen. I want to give you this before we go in, okay?"

"And I want you. You look so sexy in this dress. It's been torture not to touch." Her gown is sleeveless—bare shoulders, her cleavage tempting me.

"Remember when we got carried away at work?"

I jerk my gaze up from her cleavage. "I love when we get carried away."

"Adrian, my husband, my hero, you can now officially add one more title to that list."

"Boss man, I know."

She laughs. "And prince, shark, and alpha. You do have a lot of titles." She beams. "I hope you'll like this one most of all —father."

"Father," I echo.

"Yes. I'm pregnant. You're going to be a dad. Do you like your wedding gift?"

I stare at her in shock. "You're pregnant." It's not like we didn't use condoms, except for that one time. "Is this from when I bent you over my desk?"

"Shhh, yes! Remember we got carried away?"

It finally clicks into place. I'm going to have a family with Sara, my wife, the love of my life. I grab her and hug her, spinning her around.

She laughs. "I take it you like your wedding gift."

"I love it! I love you!" I bend down and kiss her stomach. "And I love you, little baby."

She cups my cheek. "Everything is so perfect right now. I wish I could freeze time."

"Me too." I kiss her again tenderly. "I'm so happy."

We smile at each other for a long moment, sharing in the perfect bliss of starting on this amazing journey to marriage and family together. Suddenly I realize it's unusually quiet in the palace.

I cock my head, listening. So strange. We're not far from the ballroom, so why don't I hear our family and friends? "We should probably get to the reception. I bet they're waiting for us to start."

"Okay, but let's keep the baby news to ourselves. It's early yet. I just found out a few days ago."

"It's going to be so hard to keep it secret."

"You can tell one person, just one."

"You're only saying that so you can tell Chloe."

"That's right, and don't choose a blabbermouth to tell."

"I'll tell my mother. She loves being a grandmother, and she'll treat you like a gem the entire time."

"Deal," she says.

I open the ballroom doors and gesture for her to go ahead of me. It's still deathly quiet. I step inside to find something I never thought I'd see—

My Brooklyn cousins, all six of them standing on one side of the ballroom staring at my family on the other side. Six guys in their twenties and thirties and, I have to say, seeing them in black tuxes like my brothers, the family resemblance is strong. Tall, wide shoulders, dark brown hair, angular cheekbones, and square jaws. My uncle and aunt don't seem to be with them. I guess it's up to the next generation to make peace again.

"Omigod, they actually showed up," Sara whispers.

We invited them, after clearing it with my family, but they hadn't RSVP'd to the invitation. I didn't notice them at the ceremony. Silvia beams at me. I'm sure she had something to do with this reunion.

The butler announces, "Prince Adrian Rourke and Princess Sara Rourke."

The spell is broken, and everyone applauds.

Sara laughs. "I forgot I would be a princess. Kiss me so I know I'm not dreaming."

I kiss her and nip her lower lip. She leans into me. "You're not dreaming."

She takes my hand, and we join our family, now even larger with my Rourke cousins and our baby on the way.

I bet on us, and I won the jackpot.

Don't miss the next book in the series *Rogue Prince*! Meet the Brooklyn cousins, the rough-around-the-edges Rourke men with no intention of settling down. Dylan's story is up next, where he's about to collide with his long-time frenemy and one-time lover.

Rogue Prince

Dylan

I am the crown prince of Villroy, but instead of taking the king's throne like I should have, my father got us all exiled. I'd complain, but he had good reason. Now our once royal family lives in Brooklyn, and I'm about to inherit a new kingdom: my uncle's construction business. It's an opportunity to build my real estate empire and make something of myself. All I need is an experienced person to help take it to the next level. And then the girl who grew up next door to me—all woman now—shows up with just the business experience I need.

Too bad Ariana Bianchi hates me. I used to think it was undeserved—fall-out from our families' long-time feud—but there was this one time…

Ariana

I'm newly divorced and crashing at my parents' house until I can get my life on track for my ultimate goal of having a baby with the help of a sperm bank. It's the reason for my divorce—he didn't want kids—and at thirty-one the clock is ticking. So when the gorgeous pig of a man, Dylan Rourke, shows up at my parents' house to ask me to work as a consultant for his company, I see an opportunity. He wants something from me? Yeah, well, I want something in return, too.

Only Dylan makes this way more complicated than it needs to be.

Sign up for my newsletter to be emailed when *Rogue Prince* releases at kyliegilmore.com/newsletter

ALSO BY KYLIE GILMORE

Happy Endings Book Club Series

Hidden Hollywood (Book 1)

Inviting Trouble (Book 2)

So Revealing (Book 3)

Formal Arrangement (Book 4)

Bad Boy Done Wrong (Book 5)

Mess With Me (Book 6)

Resisting Fate (Book 7)

Chance of Romance (Book 8)

Wicked Flirt (Book 9)

An Inconvenient Plan (Book 10)

A Happy Endings Wedding (Book 11)

The Clover Park Series

The Opposite of Wild (Book 1)

Daisy Does It All (Book 2)

Bad Taste in Men (Book 3)

Kissing Santa (Book 4)

Restless Harmony (Book 5)

Not My Romeo (Book 6)

Rev Me Up (Book 7)

An Ambitious Engagement (Book 8)

Clutch Player (Book 9)

A Tempting Friendship (Book 10)

Clover Park Bride: A Clover Park Short

A Valentine's Day Gift (Book 11)

Maggie Meets Her Match (Book 12)

The Clover Park STUDS Series

Almost Over It (Book 1)

Almost Married (Book 2)

Almost Fate (Book 3)

Almost in Love (Book 4)

Almost Romance (Book 5)

Almost Hitched (Book 6)

The Rourkes Series

Royal Catch (Book 1)

Royal Hottie (Book 2)

Royal Darling (Book 3)

Royal Charmer (Book 4)

Royal Player (Book 5)

Royal Shark (Book 6)

Rogue Prince (Book 7)

ABOUT THE AUTHOR

Kylie Gilmore is the *USA Today* bestselling author of the Rourkes series, the Happy Endings Book Club series, the Clover Park series, and the Clover Park STUDS series. She writes humorous romance that makes you laugh, cry, and reach for a cold glass of water.

Kylie lives in New York with her family, two cats, and a nutso dog. When she's not writing, wrangling kids, or dutifully taking notes at writing conferences, you can find her flexing her muscles all the way to the high cabinet for her secret chocolate stash.

Thanks for reading *Royal Shark*. I hope you enjoyed it. Would you like to know about new releases? You can sign up for my new release email list at kyliegilmore.com/newsletter. I promise not to clog your inbox! Only new release info, sales, and some fun giveaways.

I love to hear from readers! You can find me at:
    kyliegilmore.com
    Instagram.com/kyliegilmore
    Facebook.com/KylieGilmoreToo
    Twitter @KylieGilmoreToo

If you liked Adrian and Sara's story, please leave a review on your favorite retailer's website or Goodreads. Thank you.

www.ingramcontent.com/pod-product-compliance
Lightning Source LLC
Chambersburg PA
CBHW071003180726
48291CB00004B/1414